The Gold Nugget

A collection of short stories
by

Maureen Sparling
Illustrations by R.J. Cullen
(Celtic designs public domain)

**Published By
Insignia Publications**
32. Singland Crescent,
Garryowen,
Limerick,
Ireland

Published in Ireland 2000
By Insignia Publications
32 Singland Crescent
Garryowen
Limerick
Ireland

c.Maureen Sparling 2000

ISBN 0 953914 0 5

All Rights Reserved. No part of this publication may be reproduced or transmitted in any form or by any means electronic or mechanical, including photography, recording or any information storage or retrieval system, without the permission in writing from the publisher. This book is sold subject to the condition that it shall not by way of trade or otherwise, be lent, re-sold, hired out or otherwise circulated without the publisher's prior consent in any form of binding or cover other than in which it is published and without a similar condition including this condition being imposed on the subsequent publisher
'The characters described in these stories are fictitious.
Any resemblances to people either living or dead
is entirely co-incidental'.

Insignia
Publications

Dedication

This little book is sincerely and deservedly dedicated to the memory of
Dairíne Byrne
Whose generous contribution to the artistic and dramatic life
of our city and further afield knew no bounds

'Bean fhíor-chumasach ba ea í'.
And
Séamus O'Cinnéide
Whose vibrant contribution to the city's historical, folklore
and cultural life in general have made their mark

'Fear ar leith, ach fós ba dhuine dínn féin é'.

Both these fine people, in their own individual way
have left deep footprints in Limerick's Sands Of Time

'Catch, Oh! Catch the transient hour,
Improve each moment as it flies,
Life's a short summer, man a flower,
He dies, alas! How soon he dies'.

From 'Two Months at Kilkee"
By Mary John Knott

Publisher's Credits
Special thanks are extended to the following
Maureen Sparling for her stories and her faith in the project, R.J. Cullen for his excellent illustrations and Eric FitzGerald (EFG music & media) for his technical expertise. Ivan Morris at McKerns Printers and all our supporters and sponsors.

Sponsors

Millennium Awards City Hall
ÉIRE

ICC Investment Bank
John Hunt-Hunt Museum
Argosea Services
Live 95FM
Michael Nash
Limerick City Arts Council
Friends of the Bard

Contents

Introduction by Mike Finn

A Golfing Goof 1

Auntie Ethel's Eiderdown 13

Journalist in Jeopardy 19

Mystery at 'The Toll House' 25

The Silvery Shining Gun* 35

The Cathedral Ghost* 42

Masie 49

Romance at 'The Mary Rose' 55

A Weird and Wonderful Honeymoon* 68

The Ingenious Curator* 72

To Find a Thrifty Wife 80

Measley's Metamorphosis 87

Twice, She Came a-Cropper* 95

Jimin 100

Who Killed 'Nettles' Normoyle? 107

*Previously Published
Twice, She Came a-Cropper, The Ingenious Curator,
A Weird and Wonderful Honeymoon, The Silvery Shining Gun, The Cathedral Ghost,
appeared in 'The Limerick Christmas Gazette'.

Introduction

For a city of its size, Limerick has produced more than its fair share of writers. A city that has seen and heard so much, is bound to have many things to say and Limerick writers have been singing the song of the city for centuries. Words flow through the town like spawning salmon and like sturdy fishermen, her writers take to the waves to catch these fertile phrases.

Shady verbs lurk in shallow pools, nervous nouns dart from rock to rock while frisky adjectives leap the Curraghgower Falls. Into these shoals of possibility, the writers of Limerick cast their flimsy nets, hauling reluctant words ashore, to be arranged and rearranged on the stalls of their imagination.

Sean O'Tuama, Michael Hogan, Kate O'Brien, Desmond O'Grady, Louie Byrne, David Hanley, Michael O'Toole, Michael Curtain, JM O'Neill, Chriostoir O'Floinn, Denis O'Shaughnessy, Michael Collins and of course, Frank McCourt are just some of the many writers who have fished here.

Maureen Sparling knows this river well and from its wordy depths she serves up a feast of stories and poetry from her cottage on King's Island. The cathedrals, churches, grave yards, castles, tollhouses, pubs and shops that form the background to so many Limerick lives, are the backdrops before which the characters in this volume play out their destinies and when the grey of the city becomes too much, the sun drenched sands of Kilkee or the lush green fields of West Clare can always be unfurled.

And what a motley collection of characters strut and fret their hour before these canvasses! Between these pages you'll find hapless golfers, beleaguered bachelors, Woodbine-chomping journalists, military ghosts, artful art dealers, formidable matriarchs, jam-making matrons, disgruntled actresses, romantic widows and short pants cowboys, not to mention the unfortunate Nettles Normoyle and the miserly Measly McGrath.

Here are love stories, ghost stories, mysteries and romances, in a book that, like Auntie Ethel's Eiderdown, will be around for years, warm and comforting and familiar and ready to reward those who look inside.

Mike Finn October 2000
(Mike Finn is author of 'Pigtown' and a member of Island Theatre Company)

A Golfing Goof

Sylvester Stundon sped past "Fanny O'Dea's" at a speed of seventy miles an hour. No, he felt, he couldn't stop today, bad luck or not. Several Limerick folk sat outside this famed landmark, consuming various beverages under God's glorious blue canopy. A sea of colourful summer wear greeted his eyes as the sun shone brilliantly on that Friday of the August weekend. Sylvester, bachelor of some sixty five-years, was a popular personality among the golfing fraternity in Limerick as well as at his favourite seaside resort of Kilkee. A few miles further on he began to wonder, "Oh Lord! Should I have stopped, they say its bad luck "On second thoughts" he said to himself, "sure that's all pishogary". The elegant silver haired well-dressed gentleman drove in haste but automatically slowed down as he entered the busy town of Killrush. He didn't drive down Vendaleur Street but he took a sneaky turn to the right, then right again "Ah!" he breathed, only eight miles to my panacea!"

Speeding by "Taylor's" in Moyasta he thought "Great sure I'm almost there. Half a mile on he was forced to slow down to thirty miles per hour.

A giant haystack appeared to crawl along the road in front of his high-tech vehicle. It was so high and yet so low to the ground that the sight of the old tractor pulling it along was completely obliterated. "Strange" thought Sylvester "even in the eighties there are still those who persist in doing things the old way. "Ah well" he mused " old habits die hard". He tapped impatiently on the steering wheel, the ever-pleasant voice of Jim Reeves came across on his radio singing what Sylvester now considered a most appropriate tune "He'll have to go". Realising there was no way he could possibly pass this monstrous mobile haystack he reluctantly decided to join the posse leisurely humming "Swing Low Sweet Chariot". A mile or two on, the road widened enabling the driver of the silver car to pass the giant mobile haystack "Thanks be to God" exhaled Sylvester as he sped on.

The driver of the old tractor was a leisurely looking chap, wearing a heavy, polo neck Aran jumper, despite the blistering heat. He extended a causal wave to the speedy driver, then returned to release his old turned-down pipe from between his lips. "Dear God!" sighed Sylvester as he glanced in his rear mirror "Is that an Aran pull-down cap he has on as well?"
As the vast, dazzling Kilkee Bay came within his view, Sylvester experienced a vibrant release of energy. It was always the same, no matter how many times a year he visited this ineffable spot he called, God's perfect aquatic acre. Although anxious to get settled in, he thought first he'd like a round of golf. But before all that he had a natural; urge to pay a visit to his local when residing in Kilkee, "O'Connell's". Pulling up outside the pub, he got out and carelessly shut the car door. Kilkee was deemed one of the safest, crime-free spots of all. Doors remained open and bikes were casually slung, unlocked, against shop fronts and lodgings here and there. "Hello Margaret! Greeted a happy-go-lucky Sylvester. "Great weather isn't it?" "Ah what! replied the friendly barmaid, "I don't remember a summer like it since seventy-six" "The usual Mags" went on Sylvester. While the barmaid fixed his double whiskey the silver haired gent leafed absentmindedly through the weekend "Limerick Leader". The door opened and in came Joe Gleeson another Limerick man "Well Sylvie " he greeted "Down for a few rounds of golf?" 'That's right' replied Sylvester taking a generous slug from his glass. Sylvester Stundon was a

most accessible and well-liked man. He had gained the reputation in the golfing circles of having a fair old swing Most of his associates were aware of his cultured lifestyle. Though he lived alone he had built up a fine collection of classical records and his library abounded in books on the greatest literary figures. The poets Milton, Byron, Burns, Moore, Allingham, Frost, and Blake, were no strangers to Sylvester's bookshelves His love of literature was clearly apparent from the names he choose for both his residences. Down in Kilkee his house over on the West End was called "Byronville" and while at home on the North Circular Road in Limerick he appropriately named his residence "Poe Haven" a name which was not greeted too kindly by certain neighbours. But how were they to be expected to appreciate Sylvester's avid interest in the dark mysterious macabre tales of his literary idol Edgar Allan Poe. This haunting American writer held Sylvester in grips of wonderment and intrigue on many winters' nights. He could never have enough of such stories as "The Fall of the House of Usher" and "The Masque of the Red Death." After a second drink, Sylvester and Joe Gleeson emerged from the pub in most salubrious form, having bade a cheery so long to Margaret. It was only six thirty with sufficient of God's natural light remaining. Want a lift? asked Sylvester. "Ok," replied Joe gratefully, "I could do with a round of golf before dinner." "I find," put in Sylvester somewhat authoritatively, "That a round never fails to make me positively ravenous." Speeding off up past the boathouse the much gruntled driver remarked "We're in for a treat of a sunset this evening by the looks of it Joe." Following a successful round of golf Sylvester drove back to "Byronville" on the West End, picking a half pound of cold sliced turkey and a fresh loaf of bread in "Nolan's." Later that evening Sylvester enjoyed the musical talent at 'Bayview' among a host of friends and acquaintances.

Early on the following morning, six-thirty to be precise, a tractor was busy down on the strand, shifting amounts of seaweed that was wont to gather at one particular spot on the West End. It was in the vicinity of the high wall, where certain holidaymakers enjoyed many lively games of ball with their tennis rackets within sight of the Diamond Rocks. Dan Haugh worked away steadily, shifting load after load of the slivery, gangly soaking seaweed. Then suddenly and without warning, among the final batches of residual seaweed, he spotted what appeared to be a huddled clump of clothes. "Looks like the tide stole a march on someone's clothes yesterday" he said to himself. However, upon further investigation, the shocked and puzzled tractor driver learned that inside the huddled clump of clothes was a body, perhaps drowned, he thought. It was in a much frightened and flustered state that Dan Haugh made his hasty way up to the Garda station, on the East End. As yet, at this very early hour, no human had emerged. Knocking violently on the door, Dan heard the roar of impatience "Who the blinkin' hell could that be at this hour?" Garda Justin Talty, a well built man of some six foot two, emerged in somewhat of a scruffy condition. "Garda, Garda" blurted out Dan "A body, clothed washed up over the West End" "Oh God," said Guard Talty in a much reformed tone. "That's terrible news, terrible indeed" Dashing back inside for his keys Guard Talty alerted Guard Pierce Nolan. Both of them lost no time in sitting into the garda car with the bewildered messenger, breathless in the back seat. In a matter of minutes all three had descended the slip and were carefully observing the sombre scene. In a most officious manner, Guard Talty produced a rather tattered slim notebook from his left breast pocket. He then began to make notes with a small led pencil on the first empty page; male of small stature, stout build, scarce of hair, black leather boots, lace of left boot missing, around sixty-five, rough guess. "What's this?" observed Guard Nolan, "A gash by the left temple" "Probably inflicted from behind." put in Talty " A left handed person without doubt" he continued, his investigative mind brimming at the surface. Summoning an ambulance from Ennis General Hospital , the victim was swiftly brought there for further examination. The State pathologist was brought in

Meanwhile down near Doolin, a distraught Miko Gorman was beside himself with worry and frustration. His brother, Pajoe, was nowhere to be found. Two weeks back, unbeknown to Miko, he had had a run in with Big John Hayes a burly uncouth farmer a mile or so down the road. He and Pajoe shared acreage bordering on each other. Big John claimed that Pajoe had swiped one of his haystacks. A row, which became rather heated ensued. Pajoe known the country 'round for his uprightness and honourable ways, had taken great umbrage for no such man wishes to be accused of wrongdoing.

Later that evening Guard Talty, puffing slightly followed Guard Nolan half way up the famous ascent of George's Head. Between them they had presumed the body must have been thrown from a height. A few paces from the verdured pinnacle they spotted a silvery object of some length beside a cluster of mushrooms. Pacing forwards, Guard Nolan, the fitter of the two stood looking down at the object. He did not pick it up but gently moved it around with his size ten shoe. "A golf club," he concluded rubbing his chin, "Strange place for a golf club what?" "Quite so," commented a rather winded Justin Talty, " Must have been a golfer, " he concluded finally. "We'll find out," said Guard Nolan "A left handed one at that"! he continued. Placing a plastic bag about the bare tip of the golf club, Guard Talty placed it in a special container. They both descended the Head, much happier for their investigative prowess so far, yet debating slightly as to which of them had spotted the silver object first. A few yards beyond the little wooden bridge they sat into their car and took off at a speed unprecedented in that peaceful patch of lofty cliffs and time worn crags. Back at the station word had gone come through that the victim, now known to be a certain Pajoe Gorman, had been cudgelled by an instrument, possibly iron and administered by a powerful left-handed person, that is if the blow came from behind. In the event that the blow came from the front, then the murderer could have been right–handed. The time was now ripe for the busy and knowledgeable guard to pay a visit to the local golf club. Sure weren't the initials "S.S." clearly imprinted on the deadly murderous, albeit, silver coated instrument? The rest was going to be plain sailing or so they thought…Confidently approaching the secretary of the club, they requested to see a list of names of the regular attendees. A dutiful index finger of Garda Nolan pursued the endless list. Mullins, Naughton, Pomeroy, Reals, Saunders, Simms, Stundon. Here the guard's finger paused, Sylvester Stundon… proof perfect, most certainly the culprit. But first they must do a bit of groundwork, conduct an investigation, find out what type of character this "S S" was. They had his address in Killkee "Byronville" on the West End. They were familiar with the house but not the owner or occupant, That afternoon, as the various golfing enthusiasts drifted happily into the bar following their various rounds of golf on the pitch, the two gardai got busy in earnest. Just by coincidence, on that particular day Sylvester had planned a trip to Ennis. Occasionally he liked to browse around the Saturday market. "What type of man is he this Sylvester Stundon?" queried Guard Talty, "A grand man really" replied Connor O'Brien "The kind you could trust with your life." "Is that so now?" observed the guard, giving a knowing wink to his colleague. "Very cultured, and" reported Joe Hayes, "He loved literature especially the works of Edgar Allan Poe, you know the fella who wrote about finding bodies built into stone walls of old houses." " Ah yes," went on Hayes "He loved telling us about that one so he did." "I'm sure he did," put in Justin Talty. "A master of the art of camouflage, I'd say too". "Oh without a doubt," put in Pierce Nolan as they walked out and into their car. "Is he ever in for a shock," said one to the other 'This opera loving silver haired golfer." Pulling up outside "Byronville," both men were quick to observe the absence of a car in the avenue, though they did take note of a large bathing towel strewn lazily across the garden seat. A bathing togs lay flung on the window sill to the right "Must have been out for an early morning dip," said Garda Nolan. "Yes," replied Talty putting on a brave face, "Can't be up to these city slickers can you" "No indeed," drawled Nolan "You can't." Upon discreet investigation they learned from a neighbour that Mr Stundon had gone away for the day and he wasn't sure where. "Great" blurted out Talty, "All this is adding up very nicely, very nicely indeed." It was almost dusk that Saturday evening when Sylvester Stundon arrived back at his Kilkee residence . He had enjoyed his day in Ennis, had contacted his old friend , Jude Mansfield, the bagpipe player and had a few drinks. "What's this" he said to himself blinking twice " A garda car, wonder what's up?" Before he knew it, Sylvester was approached by the two six foot men in garda uniform. "Mr Stundon," broached Guard Talty "We'd like to ask you a few questions." "Sure surely" replied Sylvester obligingly. Once inside the house, questions fired like shooting sparks from a forge. "You're an avid golfer right?" inquired Nolan. "Yes," replied Sylvester completely bewildered. "And you're left handed I understand," put in Talty. "How did you… yes," replied the much confused gentleman, faltering somewhat "That's fine," continued Guard Talty " And you left this town early this morning, where were you may I ask?" "I wanted to attend the market in Ennis and contact a friend or two while there," replied Sylvester. "How very convenient," said Nolan, his eyes down and smiling to himself. "May I be permitted to ask," queried Sylvester eventually, "What is all this questioning about?" "Time and time alone will reveal all" replied Guard Talty " Tell me," pursued Guard Nolan in an officious manner, "How many golf clubs do you have?" Without even stopping to think, the much flummoxed man replied, "Why, six clubs, I have had the selfsame six clubs for nearly three decades now." "Is that so?," said Talty inflecting the final word, " Could we see them maybe?" "Yes of course," replied Sylvester obligingly. As they walked out to the car garda Nolan queried "Is it true you have a love of that master of the macabre, Poe, yes?" Completely taken off guard, Sylvester replied, "Yes, but what on earth has this to do with?" "Time will reveal all," replied the crafty guard. Confidently opening the boot of his silver car Sylvester pulled out the caddy bag containing his golf clubs. Guard Talty was first to observe, "Five clubs, only five." "But," protested the puzzled gentleman, "I can't understand, someone must have…" "You're coming with us," snapped Guard Nolan, "Right now Mr Stundon." Poor Sylvester Stundon didn't know what had hit him. Before he knew it he was landed at the East End of his favourite seaside resort, inside the garda station, handcuffed! Such excitement had never before been experienced at this tranquil resort. The following day up at the local golf club Sylvester's presence was greatly missed. All the investigative prodding the previous day had given rise to a certain speculation "Do you think something happened to him?" queried Joe Gleeson "I hope not," replied Hayes, "Sure Sylvie is one of the most colourful characters around here." Concern was rife. Few were in any great form for a game. Most just sat there hugging their glasses of Guinness or whiskey or orange. Back at the station, misfortunate Sylvie sat pre-judged by the two crafty guards. He found himself totally helpless and completely immersed in a cauldron of puzzling insensitivity. They didn't even think to offer him a glass of water.

Meanwhile down in the idyllic village of Doolin, word was beginning to filter through to the distraught and shocked inhabitants that Pajoe Gorman's body had been washed ashore on Kilkee strand in the early hours of the previous day. The weapon, without the shadow of a doubt, an iron golf club. Miko was simply inconsolable. Below in the valley in a two-roomed cottage, a wee man Tomas Cotter cogitated with himself as he puffed on his clay pipe. He kept his front and back door tightly shut. He wanted no interruptions. But hadn't he seen Big John Hayes remove a long object covered with newspaper from his car on Friday evening? He shook himself in an effort to remember every detail. Tomas was seventy eight. Now, he wondered who would believe a man of his age, probably say he was doting. Being a very private man of astute judgement and delicate conscience, Thomas knew exactly what he saw but decided to speak to no man concerning the matter. Down at the local that night he kept his well-trained ear to the ground. "They say" he overheard "They say they have the man, a Limerick swank.". "Not sure of the motive," added Ted O'Grady "But," said Paschal Doyle. "They have proof positive of the murder weapon, an iron golf club, it even had your man's initials on it. Poor, poor Pajoe, the very salt of the earth.". Strangely enough, Thomas noticed the absence of Big John Hayes. All this was adding up and was supplying him with a fine sharpening stone upon which to edge his verbal knife. "He's to be tried at a special hearing of Ennis District Court on the coming Monday at twelve noon." On that note Thomas rose, placed his glass on the counter in gentlemanly fashion and quietly left unnoticed, supported by his fine old blackthorn stick. As he proceeded down the valley to his cottage, few there were who knew of the vital information that this aged, limping man, possessed. Meanwhile back in Kilkee, not one of Sylvie's golfing friends were aware of his inexplicable predicament below at Kilkee Garda Station. Sunday, being the following day, Thomas Cotter attended Mass as was usual but instead of going to the pub afterwards he went straight home and tightly shut his door, bolting it securely. There, within his own four walls he planned on his movements for the following day. One thing was certain in his mind. He could not stand by and see an innocent man accused in the wrong. Meanwhile in and around the village, Big John Hayes kept a very low profile.

At eight o'clock on Monday morning, Thomas tackled up his faithful donkey, Dobbins and started out on the long trek to Ennis. For Thomas, this was a most necessary and important errand. A matter of good versus evil and a grave matter of conscience. None of the villagers had started out yet and that suited Thomas very well. Arriving in Ennis with plenty of time to spare, he tied Dobbins up at the Square and asked Mrs. O'Connor over at the newsagency to keep an eye on her. He had brought along a bale of hay and he laid it down well within her reach. Biding his time, he then strolled around the town taking great interest in the windows of the hardware shops. At about quarter to twelve he made his way to the Courthouse, where the trial of Sylvester Stundon, the swanky city golfer, was about to begin. He could tell from the line of cars outside the men who were already inside. Quietly, Thomas found himself a seat near the back of the courtroom and on the outside. All had been pre-planned on the previous day. All rose when the judge and his attendees entered. Sylvester Stundon stood on trial for the murder of Pajoe Gorman, an honest upright, and hard-working farmer from Doolin. The weapon was produced, the letters S.S. denoting identity with the owner, Sylvester Stundon. "How do you plead?" queried the stern-faced wigged Judge, Stubbs by name. "Not guilty!" came the fine cultured voice of the silver-haired gent. "Where were you on the night in question?" pursued the judge. "After a few drinks at "Kett's" I went home to bed." replied Mr Stundon. "And" continued the judge in taunting manner, "When did you realise you were minus one golf club?" "When I went to the boot of my car with Garda Nolan and Garda Talty," replied Sylvester. "Is that so now," went on judge Stubbs, his face almost creasing into a dismissive leer, "Did you not play a round the previous day?" he continued. "Yes, I most certainly did," replied Sylvester in a definite and very commanding tone. "And you meant to say you didn't miss your golf club then?" judge Stubbs continued to taunt " No, I didn't " replied the accused "My regular caddy takes care of all my needs in that respect." "Is that so?" remarked the ferret-eyed, overweight judge "We have servants then have we?" It gave Thomas Cotter all he could do to keep from shouting "Bloody injustice," at the judge. Instead as pre–meditated he caught the eye of Stundon's solicitor, Peter Hodkinson by name. Following a certain amount of whispering, the relieved solicitor informed the judge that an elderly man at the back wished to say something. Hobbling up from the back with the aid of his blackthorn stick, Thomas Cotter bravely took the his stand in the witness box, having (quite unnecessarily in his case) sworn to "tell the whole truth and nothing but…so help him God." "What can a doting old man of his age have to add to the case?" whispered Stubbs to Hodkinson "I don't know," whispered Hodkinson to Stubbs, " I only just met him now for the first time." "And what have you to say Cotter?" enquired the judge. Thomas Cotter cleared his throat and in full voice began, "Your honour, it was on a Friday evening last about eight o clock to be exact, I saw Big John Hayes arriving outside his house. I was on my way to a house down in the valley at the time I'm very sure of that. "And" interrupted the judge in a rather hostile tone. "Is Big John Hayes a friend of or foe of yours?" " "He's neither," replied Cotter bluntly. "Continue then" went on the judge passively "I saw this man remove from his cart a long object covered with newspaper" added the elderly man. By this time all those present were aghast and curiosity oozed out from every nook and corner of the packed courtroom. Beckoning for the golf club to be brought forward the judge then queried, " Was it about that size would you say?" "It was just that size," replied Cotter. The judge then ordered the elderly man to step down. "Find out exactly where that man lives" Sylvester Stundon whispered to his solicitor. "I will be glad to," replied Hodkinson. A buzz of noisy chatter now filled the courtroom. Bringing down his mallet firmly, judge Stubbs shouted, " Silence!" He then continued " This court is adjourned until Friday at twelve noon." By this time Thomas Cotter had left unnoticed. By the time the others had visited their favourite hostelries to thrash out the court proceedings over a drink or two, the elderly man was well on his way back to his cottage down in the valley of his beloved Doolin. He had done his part. He was happy for that.

On the Friday of that week, the same procession of cars made its curious concerned way from Doolin to Ennis. Thomas Cotter stayed home. He remained indoors and kept his cottage door shut. He breathed a prayer for Sylvester Stundon, a man whom he had now come to respect, for all the right reasons. At precisely twelve noon, the court again rose out of respect for the judge. With head bent, a very much shaken Big John Hayes on request approached the witness box. "How did you spend last Friday?" queried the now much enlightened judge. "I went to Kilkee for provisions for my house and farm," replied the accused rather grumpily "And while there did you go anywhere near the golf club by any chance? continued the judge. "No your honour," replied the accused "I'm too busy for them fancy places." Judge Stubbs allowed himself a grimace. Sylvester was then questioned as to whether or not he had secured his car door and boot when he went to "O'Connell's" for drinks on that particular day. To which query Sylvester replied, "No, Killkee has the much envied reputation for strict honesty and is completely devoid of all thievery." Judge Stubbs then questioned Big John Hayes at length concerning his past association with the murdered man Pajoe Gorman. It finally emerged following much professional prodding on behalf of the judge and solicitor Hodkinson that things were far from amicable between the pair. "Isn't it true?" taunted judge Stubbs "that when you went to Killkee for your provisions on the day in question you had murder on your mind?" "I don't know I don't know," shouted Big John, obviously realising he was caught out. Following this outburst the accused broke down and out spilled the entire gruesome story. Inside the packed courtroom a pin could be heard to drop as Big John, mid sobs of regret told his gruesome story. It emerged that, yes, the accused spotted some golf clubs protruding from the boot of partly locked car boot outside the said pub opposite "Bayview," the which weapon he conveniently swiped and carefully concealed in common newspaper. That evening around half eight or a bit beyond that time, when he knew Pajoe drove his tractor to Kilkee to check his stock up at George's Head, Big John pursued the stocky farmer from a distance. Using the golf club as a kind of walking stick, he disguised his appearance somewhat, wearing a topcoat, which he normally never did, and a souwester, thus completely altering his appearance. As Pajoe Gorman mounted his appointed spot Big John Hayes crept up behind him and cruelly dealt his fatal blow. Being conveniently close to the edge it was little trouble for a man of Big John's bulk to throw the body over making it look as if the deceased had drowned. "The saddest part of this entire case, is the fact that it was all over a common haystack," Judge Stubbs reminded the mute court. Many, especially those of the older men sat tear-filled. They could hardly believe that hatred could go to such lengths, Despite the extreme sadness of situation it had served to teach one and all a dear dear lesson.

When things had subsided in the ensuing days, Sylvester Stundon drove down to Doolin to visit Thomas Cotter. He owed his reputation to this elderly farmer and within a short time they were fast friends. Every year after that Sylvester Stundon visited the old farmer down in Doolin. But never once did he make the trip to Kilkee again without stopping at the old landmark, "Fanny O Dea's" even if he were only to buy a box of matches. The one and only time he did pass it out it proved that bad luck most certainly had followed.

Auntie Ethel's Eiderdown

Ethel Grieg lived in a delightful 17th century bungalow called "My Little Acre" a little way up the Dunlicky Road, just outside the peaceful, scenic town of Kilkee. A slim medium sized woman, she had lived alone in this house since the death of her father, Ambrose, twenty years previously. Her mother Minnie had preceded him by about five years. The name Grieg was a great source of intrigue and wonder to the inhabitants of Kilkee and to the people of the neighbouring county who had occasion to come into contact with the family. Some maintained it was a mistake on the original birth certificate while others were of the opinion that a foreign ship landed at Moneypoint during the last century. A fellow by the name of Grieg got off and later after taking a particular fancy to either the area or a lady, he never again boarded the ship.

Whatever the story the Kilkee Griegs never bothered to delve into their ancestry. Theirs had been a large family, they raised five boys Tomasín, Sean Óg, Ambrose Óg Clement and Paidín. Five girls followed, Ethel, Brenda, Máirín, Bridget and Ameilia. All with the exception of Ethel had either moved away from the old homestead or married. Some had settled as far away as Australia, others in America, and the remainder had settled in and around Country Clare. Ethel had never entertained the idea of marrying. In fact she had always considered the idea a distinct impossibility. The very idea of having to choose one man and live with him for the duration of her natural life filled her with a deep, dark, foreboding despair. In short Ethel very much enjoyed her own company. She rose each morning at seven and retired each night at ten. During the day there was plenty to occupy her about the farm She kept a nanny goat Jessie, and a Billy goat Patrick. Every day she diligently milked Jessie and once a year saw to it that Patrick performed his conjugal rights towards Jessie. She kept two pigs Pugs and Pudsy and two cats Nom and Pom. Ethel was a lady of particular exactitude and peculiar idiosyncrasies and if the truth were told, was considered to have achieved the highest degree of eccentricity. At the time our story begins, Ethel was in her seventieth year. She was hale and hearty and the reason possibly for same will emerge two sentences on. She wore her silvery-grey hair tied up in a bun and never had anyone seen it loosely hung. As a slight deviation, Ethel Grieg expertly operated her own still in an old cowshed in the back of the house where she had innocently placed a number of bales of hay piled high upon the other. These bales formed the perfect bulwark and to the would be eagle-eyed sentries of the law, appeared quite innocuous.

She made her occasional entrance simply by removing the bottom middle bale, which she had so adroitly positioned so as not to cause the rest of them to fall. Her craft at the art of making poteen was a well kept secret by at least three quarters of the population of Kilkee and its environs. She held certain prerequisites regarding the vending of her specialised acquired craft. Would be buyers must only come after sunset in Summer and only following the final gong of the Angelus bell in Winter. They must pass in a sterilised empty bottle, together with the money in exchange for a bottle of full-blown poteen. No words were exchanged during this operation and Miss Grieg would place her index finger up to her lips in a gesture of warning on the course of the exchange. She never retired at night before she had consumed a tumbler full herself, and two at weekends. As she used to say "Moderation in all things, that's my secret"

Ethel did not easily encourage friendships, either male or female. She considered friends to be a burden where conformity was the norm. She much preferred to wallow in her own idiosyncratic ways .She bore certain superiority regarding her surname. She was firmly convinced that her late father, Ambrose Grieg was descended from a line of Norwegians, prime amongst them was Edvard Grieg, the great composer of music. To wit, she played every evening from six to ten on her old wind up gramophone, the piece entitled "Morning" and on the reverse side of her twelve inch prized possession, a piece entitled "Peer Gynt." If by chance anyone overhearing the sweet and gentle music did enquire, Ethel would politely inform them, "Oh that's just one of the many pieces composed by my most talented ancestor Edvard Grieg" She never failed to accentuate the consonant V, so as to emphasise his nationality. This sense of superiority greatly pleased the lively septuagenarian. She never tired of listening to these two same pieces over and over again. The beauty of Ethel's simple soul was mirrored in her large brown eyes but also mirrored there if one were was astute enough to glean, dwelt a mind expertly skilled in the foolish and meandering ways of human nature, which now brings me to the kernel of my story.

Among the few valuable possessions bequeathed her by her good parents was one most authentic green feather eiderdown. Though fierce gales did blow ever so sharplyand temperatures reached below zero, none that slept beneath this prized possession ever felt the slightest chill. To this end therefore and in order to keep up contact with members of her family she decided to part with it. In and around county Clare, she was aware of three brothers who were married Paidin, Clement and Sean Og. All three visited her every Christmas Eve. Ethel decided that upon the marriage of a niece or a nephew they would be given the precious green eiderdown as a gift. It would therefore according to her wishes be passed on one to the other. It was her firm belief and she told them so, it might very well bring them good luck some day. The first to marry was Sean Og's son Ernie. Ernie married a very good and domesticated girl by the name of Matilda O'Connor. They very gratefully accepted the gift of the green eiderdown and relished its warmth on many cold winter nights.

How sorry they were therefore upon the wedding of Clement's daughter Jane to Ferdie Hannan to have to part with it. Jane and Ferdie welcomed the gift of the green eiderdown with all the dutiful and gracious appreciation which was expected of them. Miss Grieg would inform each couple upon receiving it that if she were to die while the eiderdown was in their possession then they were to keep it forever. She said no more. It so happened that eight years on Paidin's son Richard married Graham Dooley's daughter Harriet. The Dooleys were real estate agents in and around Clare for decades. So it was hardly surprising that Graham saw to it that his daughter got a great send off. A huge reception was held at the Victoria Hotel .

Harriet never took too kindly to Auntie Ethel's old green eiderdown. First of all she hated the colour green and secondly she pleaded being allergic to down feather, but the real fact of the matter was she was a snob of the highest degree. Richard was at his wit's end and didn't know how to deal with a very delicate situation, which involved his own family. It happened one day that both he and Harriet visited Auntie Ethel's house to buy a good laying hen. "And how's that green eiderdown?" she enquired " Keeping ye warm on the cold winter nights is it?" "Oh, Yes," laughed Richard. Harriet remained silent and shot a look bordering on derision to the now slightly bent old lady. Ethel copped on immediately to the younger woman's unspoken words, which lay hidden beneath that caustic look. As the couple departed she admonished "I tell ye, someday that eiderdown will bring ye luck." Needless to say on the journey home with Petulia, their newly acquired laying hen, verbal sparks flew, so much so that it was a great wonder that the old yellow volks didn't go up in flames.

About a month later it happened that a beggarman came by their house soliciting anything that the good lady of the house might have to spare. "Anything," he pleaded "And I'll pray for you good lady". Richard was at work, Harriet thought slyly, as here is the perfect opportunity. I'll tell Richard it caught fire and despite my best efforts I couldn't save it. And so without a grain of guilt she handed over Auntie Ethel's eiderdown to the old beggarman. When Richard returned from work that evening

Harriet related the tragedy of the old green eiderdown to him. He was dumbstruck at first and then upraided her for being so careless. Harriet sobbed the necessary amount of crocodile tears for appearance's sake and although Richard had his suspicions he never let on. One year onwards almost to the very hour, Auntie Ethel died. A month later the will of the good lady was read. His uncle Sean Og informed Richard that the solicitor had requested his presence for the reading of Ms Grieg's will. Richard wondered but happily complied with the request. During the reading of the will the reason for Richard's presence emerged. It seems that Auntie Ethel had sewn inside the folds of the old green eiderdown the sum of five hundred pounds, comprising of fifty, twenty, and ten-pound notes. Since Richard and Harriet were in possession of the eiderdown at the time of her death, they were to be the sole beneficiaries of the five hundred pounds. Richard sat there livid as the ghost of Hamlet's father. What was he to do? How could he explain? Then to compound an already inextricable and awkaward situation, uncle Seán Og asked him as a special request to give him the old green eiderdown after he had retrieved the money from inside the folds and Harriet had reswewen it. Richard tried to tell him but failed miserably.

When Richard returned home he related the matter of the will to Harriet. The look on her face said it all. She was shell-shocked. Richard pressed her on her most uncharacteristic disquiet. Conscience eventually pricked her and amid sorrowful tears she blurted out the whole sad, sorry story. Poor Richard could hardly believe his ears. For the first time since marrying he realised he was dealing with a snob of a wife, a proper little spoilt brat, is what he had justifiably called her. Harriet lived to rue the day she had ever parted with Auntie Ethel's old green eiderdown.

Meanwhile, Barney the beggarman, as he was affectionately known locally had moved up the country. He eventually travelled around with a circus troupe, where he worked as 'Mr Fix everything that goes wrong.' He became very attached to the old green eiderdown and carried it with him wherever he went. Then one morning he was awoken at a most unsociable hour to find a mouse tugging with all his might at the old eiderdown. So intent was the mouse on what he was doing and undaunted by

Barney coming upon him that the old beggarman decided to investigate matters. He could see very little in the gloom of the night so he decided to light the old oil lamp. It was then that he noticed the mouse scurrying off out a tiny hole in the bottom of the caravan door. He appeared to be clutching a particle of reddish paper in his mouth, Barney scratched his head and confusedly looked from the disappearing mouse to the eiderdown and back again. He flopped on his knees on top of the eiderdown to investigate further. He ripped open the gap where the mouse had been nibbling. To his surprise and delight an abundance of fifty, twenty, and ten pound notes came flying out, one tenner being slightly bitten. The puzzled beggarman sat completely flummoxed in the middle of the eiderdown, surrounded by so much paper money that he had never in his life dreamed was ever possible. Poor Barney hadn't remembered a happier day in his life since his First Holy Communion when he had collected the princely sum of two half crowns and a sixpenny bit.

Journalist in Jeopardy

It was a miserable, murky November night. For most good citizens it was the perfect night for crouching 'round the fire with a cup of hot cocoa while listening to a play on Radio Eireann. But, for one citizen at least, the fire, the cup of hot cocoa or even the story on radio, bore no attraction whatsoever. For, adjacent to the Glentworth hotel, within view of the spectacular Tait's Clock, a dim light was still visible at the unsociable hour of 12.30 a.m. Inside this vast, grey stone, church-like building sat a very perturbed man. Now in his early thirties, Ollie Brennan, who had begun on the bottom rung of the journalistic ladder, now found himself top dog in that same field. His colleagues looked up to him, so much so that he felt under constant pressure to produce good stories, to ferret out the real news in his native city. The "Limerick Weekly Echo" was a great little seller. It was, what one might refer to as "the people's paper," with regular features, such as "Inside by Outside", poems with a local flavour by a bus conductor named Daniel Joseph MacCauley, and another weekly offering by "Simple Simon". The newspaper took pride of place in just about every household of the treaty City.

Ollie sat hunched in front of his old typewriter, beads of sweat bedecked his worried, furrowed brow, beneath a crop of mousy, dishevelled hair. His short sleeves were rolled up, revealing two very paler than pale arms.

His sleeveless, Fair Isle jumper, a Christmas present from his mother five years previously, was beginning to wear thin. Didn't he well remember overhearing her telling Mrs Murphy next door, "Oh, I always shop at 'Beecher's' nothing but the best is good enough for my Ollie. This 'Beecher's' product now had two noticeable darns in its front. Ollie had a habit of pricking the front of his jumper in nervous fashion with the point of his pencil whenever he stalled mid-sentence,. searching for just the right word. Now in typical journalistic manner, a second pencil lay uprightly cocked behind his right ear. A half smoked fag hung carelessly out of the right side of his clenched lips, half an inch of ash protruded in a near balancing act. Beside the old typewriter lay an ashtray packed to capacity with Woodbine butts and slatey ash. For a man who was considered to be always on top of his job, tonight was a major downturn.

Ollie Brennan was suffering acutely. He faced a monstrous dilemma He was torn between his love for Nora his girlfriend for the past ten years and loyalty to his calling as a truthful journalist. For that day as usual Ollie had attended the court hearing down at Merchant's Quay. It was his allotted task to bring the business back to the office and have it typed in readiness for the typesetters the following morning. Idling for time, he tapped on the letter x at least twenty times, his mind a maze of distraction. He was faced with a delicate matter of the highest order. There wasn't a human soul he could possibly discuss the matter with. In a city full of people, since the hour of twelve o' clock noon he was very much, a man alone. Before him lay the bare facts in all their nakedness, in his best attempt at shorthand. Ted Frost, a bachelor of some forty-five years, was found guilty of being drunk and disorderly on O'Connell street at 9.00 p.m. on Friday, August 3rd. The court had heard that Frost had used foul language to the civic guard while stubbornly resisting arrest. Ollie stalled on the word 'foul'. Wondering how he could water down the facts, he helplessly side glanced at his half mug of cold tea. A permanent brown scum decorated the bottom half. It was Ollie's very own mug, and it was company policy that every employee kept his or her own mug and was responsible for the washing of same. Ollie hardly ever finished his mug of tea, and when he did manage to do so, quickly only found time to give it quick rinse under a spluttering tap.

Snuffing out his fag in an agitated manner, he longed for a pint of Guinness. But of that he had as good chance as hoping the sun to shine out on this chilly November morning. Ted Frost was not particular favourite of Ollie. The problem lay in the fact that Frost was the brother of his girlfriend Nora, and therein lay his dreadful dilemma. What could he do? What should he do? He clenched a woodbine between his teeth for about the twentieth time that November morn. He was cold now, his teeth began to chatter. In desperation he wrenched the paper from the old typewriter roller. Nervously he crunched it up, and then pitched it into the already overflowing paper bin. Allowing himself a swift pull from his fag, he then inserted a clean sheet of paper. He searched and searched the deep recesses of his mind to find a way out. The idea of passing on the story to another reporter floundered on the side of cowardice. He stretched down his right hand to scratch his flea ridden right leg. A frightened mouse scurried from one side of the dingy, compact, much cluttered office, and quick as lightning exited down a familiar hole of his on the other side. He scratched his leg incessantly and hoped the flea had gone for good. 'Must be that so and so Billy Tuite,' he said to himself. 'That messenger boy always bringing in his hungry for a bite flees'. Word had gone round that the same boy slept with his old sheep dog, Tucker. 'Next time I must remember to bring along the DDT' he muttered. 'Ted Frost, Bachelor, aged forty five, sentenced to four'…Ollie covered his right hand over his left fist and gritted his teeth 'Oh God what am I to do?' He breathed helplessly. 'Nora will never look at me again. Everyone knows that I am the one who works on court cases.' He was getting numb. He had to think fast. In no way could that story reach the newspaper. But the trouble lay in the fact that Jones, the chief editor, was already privy to the story.

He stood up and went to the entrance door for a breather. Tait's Clock struck out one –thirty to a sleeping city. Never before had that same clock sounded so terribly lonely. Ollie gave a sigh. What excuse could he offer his worried mother for being out so late? Having scoured his mind for a way out, he returned indoors again. He looked at the box of matches lying beside his empty packet of Woodbines. 'Ah' he thought, 'There lieth the fuel that could well rid me of my dreaded problem.' Just a few papers, he thought, couldn't I just light a few papers? He was working late. It would look innocent enough. Almost as quickly as the thought was conceived it bore fruit. Ollie Brennan slipped back into his coat and trod his weary footsteps out the back way. It was pitch dark and as he groped his unsure way his foot slipped and he took a tumble downwards, to where, he did not know. He was only familiar with the front part of the building. Ollie knew no more Meanwhile, fiery flames completely engulfed the front part of the building until eventually, one of the Dominican priests next door who was making upon an office he had skipped from the previous day, spotted the flames and immediately alerted the fire brigade. The fire was quickly brought under control but not before it had had its ravenous, flaming, roaring way. The swift action of the brave fire fighting men kept the fire from spreading to the machinery room in the back part of the building.

The following morning as they arrived for work, shock registered on the grim faces of each and every employee. 'Jones' queried Justin Mansfield the managing director 'were you the last one out last evening?' 'No' replied Jones 'I left Ollie after me, said he had a lot to catch up on.' 'Well there's no sign of him now' said Mansfield 'and he hasn't turned up for work either'. 'Do you think?'…Mansfield half queried. 'I don't know, I hope not' replied Jones in almost concerned manner. 'I don't know, I don't know' repeated Jones as he thought of his lost precious bits and pieces, as well as his prized typewriter, the best in the whole crummy office, he assured himself. It had the ability to underline in red, a very necessary addition he used to say, when trying to emphasise a point.

As the days passed, it was surmised that poor Ollie has perished in the fire, probably nodded off through sheer over-exertion of the mind, and the customary old fag still alight. His poor mother was broken-hearted. 'Oh my Ollie' she wailed 'He died in the call of duty, just as he would have wanted.' Justin Mansfield was gravely upset. He partly blamed himself for allowing his employees to smoke freely. While somewhat aggrieved, Nora shook the sad event off quickly and started going out with Gus Foley, an accomplished organist at the parish church. Within a week, the front office was almost back to normal. It was Thursday; the time was seven–thirty in the evening. Willie Whelan, the machinist, had just shut off the printing machines and was grateful to be able to hear himself thinking again. 'That's strange,' he muttered to himself. 'I thought I heard a groan of some sort'. Everyone had gone. He was alone. Just as he was about to switch off the light he was again alerted by the groaning sound. Moving in the direction of the sound he found that it seemed to come from the cellar. Descending the rather steep stairs, the groans seemed to get closer and closer. 'Help Help!' he heard. "Oh God!" he thought. "Could that possibly be Ollie down there?" Upon reaching the final step, his eyes happily fell on the stretched out figure of Ollie Brennan. 'Oh, thanks be to God' breathed Whelan. 'Help me up will you' gasped Ollie. 'I'm dying for a pint of Guinness'. Willie Whelan gave chuckle, while under his breath he murmured, 'Nothing will ever change this chancer'. 'Well I wouldn't doubt you anyway,' joked Willie. 'Everyone thinks you're dead that you perished in the fire' he went on, 'Jones has typed the first draft of your obituary. You should hear all the nice things he said about you. You'd hardly even recognise yourself.' 'Is that so now,' blinked Ollie disbelievingly. 'And to think I was envious of him and his position.' 'There you are now,' laughed Whelan. Lifting up Ollie Willie helped him to the stairs. Outside of being a little weak he seemed alright, 'We'll have to contact your mother first' said Whelan 'Then after you get a proper bite to eat, we'll head off over to the 'Widow Week's'' for a good old bout of drinking. You deserve it. After all it isn't every day a man has the privilege of reading his own obituary.'

Brennan's mother almost fainted upon seeing him. 'Oh Ollie' she wept 'My little boy Ollie. I prayed for the good Lord to bring you back and now my prayer is answered'. She cooked him sausages, pudding, tomatoes, and eggs on the pan and made a pot of tea. She even went to the shop for a fresh cottage loaf. One might say it was a celebratory meal. After eating Ollie cleaned himself up and off with himself and Willie like two bees over to the 'Widow Week's' on Patrick Street. Pushing open the door, what an unexpected surprise awaited poor Ollie. For there over in the corner, was his own beloved Nora, his cherished girlfriend of ten years standing, with her arm around Gus Foley, the holy organist from the parish church. Nora almost fainted and would have done so only that she was seated. 'Oh Ollie' she said apologetically 'I thought you were dead. Gus was even going to play for your mass next Saturday.' Ollie looked puzzled. Then she continued "I was on the point of telling you last week anyway, Ollie. You see Gus and I love each other very much. We were only waiting for the chance and when it came …well". 'Well I'll be darned' said Ollie going over to join Willie. 'I should have bloody gone and let that story go through'. 'What's that' asked Willie somewhat confused. "Ah nothing" replied Ollie grumpily as he reached over and lashed into his pint of Guinness.

When a much distraught Ollie told his mother the following day about Nora, she replied "Well now Ollie that could be all for the best. I never liked her anyway. She was too cute in her ways for you. In fact I was always hoping you'd give her a reason to break it off". "I had one" replied Ollie through clenched teeth, "I had the perfect one!"

Mystery at 'The Toll House'

It is the year 1999, summer to be exact. Down by Thomond Bridge nestled at the corner between Verdant Place and Castle Street, stands a unique stone building, with its even more unique narrow windows. It is a rather lonely building except for the odd stray pigeon that might lodge there for a night or two to recoup its energy after a significant race before flying back to its owner in some far way part of the country Now this old building had never been never been dubbed with any other degree of notoriety great or small, its common use during the last century, was that of paying a toll for the privilege of crossing over Thomond Bridge, that is until the time our story begins.

Since its closure a few decades previous, its one and only true friend has been the towering twelfth-century King Johns Castle which stood awesomely almost right across from it. Day after day it has gazed in wonder at its magnificence and was often tempted to embrace its rugged charms.

This year more especially, King John's had come into its own with visitors from far and near streaming in and out daily. On the long and lonely nights it relieved itself of chronic boredom by turning into the sometimes-gentle sometimes-masterful wild flowing Shannon River.

The turbulent Curraghgower Falls were at times a source of light relief. It could almost count each rock in the deep recesses of that ancient cavern. It rejoiced in hearing the dulcet tones of the nearby St Mary's Cathedral bellringers as they practised on Monday evenings and again it rejoiced upon hearing their mellifluous tone ring out from that self-same tower on Sunday mornings

Yet, it was not until the time that our story takes place did it realise that it possessed a restive, and ever so restive occupant. It was in fact the ghost of a lady, who failed to fulfil her potential as an actress back in the previous century. Her name was Theatrica; self-named as you may well imagine. This lady had passed away, mainly due to an over-indulgence of a certain spirit, whisky to be exact, in July 1899, just three months following the death of Michael Hogan, the Bard of Thomond.

Legend had it that she used to help out at a certain ale house on Castle Parade and thus developed her taste for the oul drop by means of sneaking a wee tipple here and there. Legend also held, that in the final score of her years (she lived to be ninety) she was rarely seen without her clay pipe. I suppose one could say it was her way of relaxing with the ever-increasing pace of life back then!. Now, exactly one century after her death, she decided to return to her native city in an almighty effort to vent her unfulfilled theatrical spleen on a handful of misfortunate, struggling actors belonging to a group called "Island".

Our frightening episode begins one Friday night in July 1999. It had been a particularly cold wet and windy July day (it happens that way in Limerick sometimes you know!). The night proved deadly with one of the highest tides witnessed so far that year. The pretentious, would-be ghost actress anticipated a secret delight in wielding her lethal sword of jealousy in the direction of the three unsuspecting actors.
In the old church nearby, the one of which 'The Curse of St Munchin' was written, some members of Island were going through their paces for

their forthcoming play "Pigtown". And talking of curses, this discontented spirit had already cursed these innocent actors in her ghostly heart, if such there be. Skin, Tosselo and Green, two of whom were staunch and prominent members of the group since its very inception, took their leave and shut the graveyard gate carefully behind them. "Bloody awful night" remarked Tosello to his two colleagues. "Sure is" muttered the other two zipping their jackets up to their chins. The silent wish of all three was that the back door of at least one pub might be open. But, no such luck on this weary night and as we shall see, worse luck was to follow.

Our silent occupant had observed these three as they individually passed her lodgings over the last few weeks on their way to practise. Skin, whom she observed to be the very essence of respectability, both in gait and demeanour. Tosello though new to the City, seemed to possess a high degree of self-assurance, both theatrically and otherwise.

Then Green, a curious cock-of-the-walk type of character who sometimes had difficulty containing himself due to the possession of a residue of natural stage talent. All this self assurance, together with natural stage talent and high degree of respectability grated on her. This rasped at her lost theatrical nerve to the degree that she bore a constant aversion to actors no matter where. But the fact of finding them on her home territory really put the kibosh on it all. She prayed nightly to Satan before retiring 'Actors, actors, bad luck to the lot of them!'. But tonight there would be little sleep for the she-ghost. She had a deadly night's work in store for herself. Now over the past few weeks Theatrica had spirited herself diagonally across the cemetery, some of which lay behind part of the Toll House. And having made her way to the Church building, she would politely perch herself on one of the window sills, where she would observe and listen as the actors went through their paces. As already stated, she had well observed Skin, Tosello and Green as they each individually made their way to practise over the past few weeks. But how ecstatically delighted she was now, as she observed the three of them swing round Castle Street together. This would certainly minimise her abductive connivance.

The three actors were happily chatting away as they approached Thomond Bridge .It was a pitiful night, which was about to disintegrate into a total abyss of complete desolation for the three unaware actors.

Skin, who was flanked by his two acting colleagues suddenly drew in a sharp breath as they passed the Toll House. Instinctively he locked both his hands on to the shoulder of each of his colleagues. Automatically the three actors were stuck fast to the spot where they stood, for their ears were pierced by a mournful cry like that of a Banshee. For some reason, which now seemed strange, almost all the windows of this odd building were either broken or missing for some months previous to this event. Then Green, by far the most outgoing of the three, finally ventured a few steps to the right and began to peer inquisitively into one of the shattered windows. Although a vigorous shivering shook his entire body, yet he was compelled to seek further. Before he knew it, he was swiftly whisked by what means he knew not into the weird, unused building.

Skin and Tosello felt duty bound to seek out their colleague, whose act they thought quite precocious and unwise. After a while, the wailing abated somewhat, and then continued again, until a pattern emerged. Peering in the shattered windows, they now began to wish they had gone home by Nicholas Street. As they each in turn still wondered about this possibility, they were suddenly suctioned into the strangely shaped stone enclosure. It was an experience akin to young Dorothy in the "Wizard of Oz" only much much worse. The scene was black as coal, the feeling was ice cold. All three were dumbstruck! Then they heard a loud, cackling laugh like that of a witch followed by a shrieking voice, which domineeringly announced

"I have a crooked leg,
And I have a crooked hand,
And if ye don't obey me
In my dungeon ye will land!"

Then all was deadly quiet. A second later they could hear each other's gasp. What were they to do? What could they do? They were trapped good and proper. Then , following some deadly mournful intonations, she set about her business of incarceration in earnest. She grabbed hold of Skin with a strength that would do justice to Goliath, shrieking all the while "Aha, aha so you are the great Sergeant Fogarty are you, frightening the life out of good people, listening in the neighbourhood lanes so that poor misfortunate man can't even have a decent row with his wife. Yes, there you are, planted with your notebook and pencil, an excuse for a pencil if you ask me. 'Tis so small if you pared it 'twould vanish, just like you're going to very soon, aha, aha, Sergeant how are you, in my day sergeants were what one would call sergeants, not sequestered spies the likes of you". Despite her obvious pre-occupation and aggravation with his part in the play, Skin plucked up courage and pleaded with her saying

'Tell us truly are you the lady
That nearly drowned poor old Drunken Thady
Answer answer if you please
And give us then our just release'.

In reply, Skin was flung aside, had both his legs tied with strong rope, which were then strung to the highest rafter of that quaint building.

Tosello was next in line for punishment. "You! who do you think you are?" she shrieked, as poor Tosello gazed at her through the dimness in utter disbelief. "Why" he ventured haltingly, "What have I done, I only love acting please let me go, please". In reply he was dragged bodily across the floor. Then she continued to vent her caustic dose on the poor bedraggled actor "An excuse for a man, that's what you are a soldier you call yourself with your tartan kilt and sailing boat hat trying to stop people going over my bridge, the cheek of you and you not even a native. That's my job you Scottish Charlatan. I've heard tell you even featured a movie 'Chameleon' I wont be long changing your colours for you, now get in there." With that, the ghost shoved poor Tosello into some sort of a trunk, which she locked and chained securely. Meanwhile, somewhere close by poor Green shook with fear, wondering what his fate would be. However, before he had time to blink, he was aware of a spirit close by. "And you Green" she taunted "The king of all actors or so you think, but as far as I'm concerned you are all foam and no beer. If it weren't for the fine speaking voice God gifted you with you'd be no good at all. A priest is it you think you are, faking bodies in coffins to get over my bridge, what kind of priest is that I ask you, a traitor to his Roman Collar, that what he is"

Poor Green squirmed in fear, all the while batting his eyelashes in a nervous gesture as he pleaded in vain with the tormentor he could not see. Paying no attention to his innocent pleadings, the ghost yanked him bodily and put him sitting on a wooden bench which was rivetted to the floor. Swiftly and without warning he was blindfolded and gagged. See no evil, speak no evil, he thought with the last vestige of humour that remained to him. Temporarily the three actors knew no more. Time stood absolutely still.

Eventually night gave way to day and day relented to evening. Normally the Island Theatre group would not have rehearsal on Saturday evening, but time was getting dangerously close and Kevlin wanted everything just right. For over a decade he had been director of and general overseer of this acting troupe. He was greatly respected. As he took the cast of 'Pigtown' through their paces, he was suddenly distracted by the obvious absence of three of his stalwarts Skin, Tosello and Green, 'Good God!' he expleted 'Where on earth can they be?' Immediately, the mobile phone went into action, but despite all his gallant efforts to locate them, he failed dismally to do so. Their families and friends proved no help at all. It was a complete puzzle, all was a fathomless source of wonder. For sure it was a conundrum to be reckoned with. And despite his normally even temperament, as the evening wore on Kevlin became abnormally agitated.

And who would blame him? After all this was to be the world premier of 'Pigtown' which was penned by Skin and who now, unbeknown to Kevlin, was hanging by ropes from rafters high up in the nearby Toll House. In just two weeks time this great theatrical extravaganza on Limerick life throughout the century, was due to expose it's unique wonder on the citizens and possibly further afield. An 'oink' party had already been held at the nearby Castle Lane Tavern to launch it's near arrival. Weren't there oink reminders over the city? And didn't the opening night promise to be one of the most outstanding events the city had ever witnessed? In short Oink was the 'in' word all over the city. But where was the fellow who started the whole oinking thing? Where was he and his two acting colleagues?

As things stood on this fateful Saturday night, grim was the 'in' word. After a futile rehearsal, the group dispersed and went their separate ways. Before departing a fellow named Christy Bryan, who actually had three parts in the play had a quick word by way of warning with Kevlin. He said how he had spotted the three missing characters turn down by Castle Street the previous night. Could it be, he related to Kevlin that they were the sad victims of a prank that went horribly wrong and ended up in the Shannon? Although, this very sensible chap was quick to add, they were most certainly old enough to know better. But that Green fellow, he added was known to take flights of fancy even as part of his normal behaviour. No, continued Bryan wouldn't trust that fellow at all, great actor but a wee bit whimsical.

Feeling more forlorn than he had ever felt in his entire life, Kevlin tentatively turned on to Castle Street. That was his way home anyway. As he approached the Toll House building he experienced what he could only describe as a numbness in his stomach, which swiftly travelled to his chest and on to his already parched throat. He thought he had heard a moaning but fright had taken such a grip on him he couldn't be sure. He never before had any reason to fear the Toll House and on that account he proceeded to negotiate the source of the moaning, which he thought he heard coming from the direction of the derelict old Toll House.

As soon as he began to peer inside the paneless window frame, his glasses fell off and fell into several broken pieces on the path where he stood. Then, before he knew it, he was landed bodily into a dark abyss. These abysmal surroundings were most certainly exacerbated by that fact that he had no glasses. Theatrica repeated her threatening four lines to the now much shocked director. Through the gloom Kevlin could just about make out the form of Skin hanging by the two legs from a rafter mainly because of his length. He heard some kind of a groan from what he thought was a large oblong coffin-like box. Then suddenly, it dawned on him that he was trapped just like his fellow actors. He couldn't speak for fright. The ghost continued to administer her warning about the dungeon in a most taunting manner. What can this spirit want thought Kevlin whose one and only business on hand was to have Pigtown staged on time. He knew that without his three colleges there could not possibly be any staging of the play.

'Aha, aha' she began, 'You bearded old blotcher, you're too tight to buy the means to shave, what are you trying to do hide the face God gave you?' She stopped momentarily. Silence prevailed for a brief space of time, then just as he was about to ask the ghost what her game was, he was witness to an almighty shriek followed by a loud clattering of what sounded like a thousand cymbals knocking off each other like dominoes. Then she issued her strong ultimatum "Give me part in your new play and I'll let ye go, if ye don't I wont!"

Kelvin was completely overwhelmed with a fear he had never before experienced. He knew he had to think very fast. He felt at that point if she had asked for the moon he would have had to find a way to fetch it for her. But, in actual fact her request to have a part in his new play was going to prove just as difficult as fetching the moon. He sorely missed consultation with his three buddies. Somehow he would somehow have to compromise. But he would have to hurry. Time was of the very essence. "Well" she shrieked "What do you say, you are the boss man aren't you?" "Give me time, please give me time" pleaded the much addled director, all the while wondering how best he was going to extricate himself from the lethal net in which he now found himself. Secretly, he prayed to every saint her never knew. There was no way of evading this shrieking female ghost. Finally, he decided to pray to the Holy Spirit. He heard around confirmation time at school that he would help to enlighten you to solve a difficult problem. But this was more, it was a serious dilemma. At last a light began to illuminate the dark recesses of his mind. Why not use her in the coffin scene. Sure, she'll be ideal for the part. Why didn't I think of that sooner?

"Well" she shrieked "What's the verdict do I get a part or don't I?" "Yes, yes" Kevlin half-stuttered. "Well I hope for your sake that your actors enunciate a little better than you, otherwise you can give 'Pigtown' the hammer" she rasped on "It'll be doomed for sure." "Oh oh yes" replied Kevlin "they speak very well indeed ,all of them' "Now about my part, I have wonderful stage potential you know.' 'You, you' Kevlin faltered 'You can replace the cabbage in the coffin'. 'Replace replace!" roared the ghost "Is that all?' 'It's the best I can do' replied Kevlin haltingly and feeling somewhat despondent at her reaction to his bright idea. 'But' he went on 'You are the most ideal person for the part, you're going to play a blinder believe me.' 'Well,' she replied, 'It's a part I suppose but I never expected my theatrical debut would consist of replacing a few heads of cabbage!'

Now without realising it, Kelvin had overed a monumental hurdle only to run into a quagmire. No, not how he would break the news to his faithful heads of cabbage, but how would he get out of the ghost taking part. Why did he give in so fast, why did he, he nagged himself. Aha, he suddenly thought Eureka! we'll take her in the coffin by the strand and …… 'You said you'd let my acting colleagues go' he said. 'No sooner said than done' she cackled happily. Their immediate release was followed by an urgent consultation with Kevlin. 'All right now' he concluded. 'We are all sure of the exact spot yes?' 'Yes', replied the other three in unison so relieved to be free from their bondage.

It was rehearsal night. For obvious reasons some props were literally walked into the Belltable Arts Centre in O'Connell Street. They went by Clancy's Strand. Lucky for them, the tide was high that evening. Just as they passed 'The Curraghgower Bar', the spot where legend holds that Drunken Thady was rescued, the members of Island were about to perform the most important act of their entire acting career to date. God help them all if they didn't get it right. This famous bar was their cue, the two in front shouldering the coffin were to conveniently stumble on a large rock, which they had purposely placed there. And so they did, and in so doing, with one almighty splash the fast flowing Shannon River received the coffin in which enclosed the spirit of Theatrica.

"Oh, God, save us all' shouted Kevlin, his pillowcase in a veritable twist, 'The coffin the coffin it's gone. I'll have to go to the undertaker for another'. Then, as if the bed was on fire, he hopped onto the floor. He immediately phoned his acting colleagues to find out if they were alright. Skin was the last one he phoned. 'I'll have to go to the undertaker' he related. 'The coffin is gone into the Curraghgower Falls'. 'Calm down' laughed Skin. 'I don't think its an undertaker you need. I know what you need but I wouldn't be saying it over the phone lest someone might hear. Tonight first stop at the Belltable, second stop for you about three quarters of a mile beyond that.' Kevlin scratched his head in reply, wonder what he means, wonder what he means? If he but knew the night I had he wouldn't be so flippant so he wouldn't. Ghosts aren't half-bad but actors can be a veritable nightmare, he thought to himself.

The Silvery Shining Gun

Tommy Small lived in a one-storey house close to St Mary's Church. He had two brothers and two sisters and they all managed to live very happy and contented in that little house, mother, father and granny Laetitia too. There was one tiny bedroom in the back of the house and another of equal size in the front part of the house, where a two –paned window let in the sunlight or appeared coated with frost, depending on the season. There was one living room, larger than the bedroom where the cooking and the eating took place. Here lay the very heart of the home, the open fire. On many a dark Autumn or Winter night, they would all gather 'round and listen to their father recount tales of long ago, tales about his travels around the country to the cattle fairs with Tommy's uncles "Ah, where's there's muck there's money" his granny would interject as she half dozed and listened while the rich glow from Reidy's finest coal burning set new highlights to her steel-grey hair. 'Ah will you whisht mother" Tommy's Dad would retort "Sure, I've seen enough muck that would fill an ocean but very little money."

Tommy's mother, Nellie, and his father, Thomas slept in the front room.

Lettie, his granny occupied the back room, where, apart from numerous holy pictures and quite a selection of rosary beads, she kept dozens of old shoes. Everyone in the house was aware of Lettie's little idiosyncrasy, that of having a fixation with shoes. Tommy, who was now only eight years old, often wondered what would happen to all the old shoes when she died. A makeshift wooden stairs led to the attic which was divided into two sections, one for girls, the other for the boys. The next in line to Tommy was his brother, Joe who was five years older than he. Joe had just started work for the busy Christmas season down the docks, bagging coal and helping John-Joe on the horse and cart to deliver it. Nellie prayed each night that he would be kept on.

The year was 1950 and it was only eight days to Christmas. Now, although Santa always visited the Small household, it seemed that he was either very scarce on toys or else he wished to teach the children a lesson on how to behave better. Either way, they very rarely got the toy they most desired. It was with this thought in mind that young Tommy had done his best to save as many pennies as he could all year to buy what his little heart desired, the silvery shining gun and holster that took pride of place in 'Poll Carr's' window at the corner of Rutland Street .His two brown eyes would light up every time he glanced at it in hopeful anticipation.

Today would be the day he'd venture in and ask how much this treasure would cost. So, off with him up the hill and down Bridge Street. It was Saturday and he had lots of time. He gave a look sideways at the Graveyard to his right but kept his eyes ahead. Might not be lucky he thought. He had heard so many different stories about the Protestants and how they didn't go to Mass and how they might not go to Heaven. As he passed the Custom House, his little heart began to thump. How much would it be he wondered, maybe two and six pence? Cusack's little shop, resplendent as usual, displayed all the signs of the festive season. Tinsel and dots of wadding made to look like falling snow, decorated a window filled with boxes of chocolate, cigars, tobacco, snuff and cigarettes.

Finally, he stood outside 'Poll Carr's' front window. "Oh!" he sighed to himself "If only I had that shiny gun, it would be like being in heaven." Slowly he stepped inside and timidly stood there waiting for Poll, who appeared lost in a maze of tinsel and toys. She raised her head when she heard the door latch click. "Well, what do you want, young fellow?" she asked in a voice that bespoke certain weariness. "Can you tell me' he quivered "How much is that gun in the window?" "Please" he added when she looked at him without saying a word. 'The gun, what gun?' she said impatiently, "There's hundreds of guns in the window." "The silvery shining one" Tommy piped up confidently, now feeling a bit more sure of his grounds. "Oh, that one" remarked Poll, her tone now mellowed somewhat, "That one is 1/3pence and if you want the holster with it will cost you 2/=." Tommy's little heart sank, he had saved only twelve penny stamps just one shilling, so if he wanted to gun he would have to get three more pennies, and he so much wanted the holster as well, the full outfit to be like John Wayne or Gary Cooper. Where would he get those twelve precious wings? Time was running out?

Despondent in heart he retraced his steps, not daring to glance to the left as he passed the cathedral graveyard. As he passed 'Dick Devane's' pub he could hear the sound of good cheer and much God save all here, despite the fact that they had opened less than two hours ago. Tommy trudged down Athlunkard Street hill, his little mind working overtime as to how he could come up with that extra money. He stopped in to say a prayer at St. Mary's Church. Father Lee emerged from his confession box and gave a knowing, sweeping glance about the church before entering the sacristy. At the back of the Church, Tommy knelt down on the wooden kneeler in front of the statue of the Scared Heart. Red nightlights flickered brightly in the dullness of the grey December day. He prayed fervently for a few minutes, then left. A few steps found him home. The smell of the backbone stew cooking gave him a momentary lift but the problem of how to come by those twelve precious pennies soon returned. As he tried to sleep that night, he tried to conjure up ways of how he might come by the extra money. He thought of the possibility of stealing two stamps from his brother's post office book but the fear of being found out put that idea firmly behind him. He even entertained the thought of stealing a pair or two of his granny's old shoes and selling them at the market but eventually conscience got the better of him.

Early the following week, Tommy got his holidays from school. Now here's my chance, he thought. He was too young to work, so he thought of doing messages for older women who lived all around him. This effort proved lucky for him and by Christmas Eve he had managed to save the extra penny stamps to get that special gun and holster.

It promised to be a very exciting day. "The cold of snow is there," his father had announced as they sat and ate their breakfast. Later that morning Tommy observed so many people passing, some with turkey's which had just been killed and plucked at the market, some others had left things a bit late and were seen carrying home Christmas Trees. More bore holly pickled with bright red berries. Many Park people could be seen making their way home on the donkey and cart, the latter packed with every kind of Christmas goodies. At about twelve noon, Tommy made a mad dash out of his front door and helter-skeltered up one hill and down the other until he reached the Post Office in a breathless state. But what a shock he got when he reached into his short pants pocket. His post-office book was gone! A hollow feeling in the pit of his stomach plus a heart that beat to overtime, set him into a sudden frenzied state as his shaking hand reached further down into a large hole in his pocket. When the reality of what happened finally registered, he burst out of the post-office and charged down the hill over Matthew Bridge, crying bitterly all the way. So terribly upset was he that he didn't even think to retrace his steps in search of his post–office book. By the time he reached 'Poll Carr's' he was breathless. Most of the guns were gone from the window but still the silvery, shining gun shone out like bright star in vast and lonely sky.

He went into the shop; his eyes blotched from crying and his body shaking with fright. He'd have to take the chance and ask her. That gun meant so much to him. 'What ails you?" asked Poll., observing the young boy's wretched state. "I, I lost my post–office book and I can't buy the silvery shining gun in the window.' Tommy punctuated his word with a sniffle . "Well, what can I do?" retorted a much-tired Poll. "Could you keep it and I might find my post- office book?" the boy timidly requested. "Now you're asking me to do a very difficult thing, I might tell you' said Poll stiffly. "Supposin' someone comes in to buy it and you don't come back." "I'll try honest I'll try,' Tommy pleaded, brightening a little. "Now if you're not back by six o' clock, I'll be closed and it's Christmas Eve you know and I won't open for god nor man nor children either" she snapped. Tommy left, feeling hopeful and gloomy at the same time.

A light snow fell gently as Tommy crossed the road. Delicious savoury smells emanated from "The Cosy" chip shop. Tommy lingered outside a while. He became hungrier and hungrier as he observed people eating fish and chips inside. The man with the pointy nose was extra busy. The vigour with which he shook the vinegar over the chips always intrigued young Tommy. For this young boy, he resembled the type of character he had heard at school from Dickens's novels. Digging his hands deep into his pockets in hopeless gesture,Tommy sauntered down the street. The sound of revelry reached his ears as he passed the porterhouse on the corner, a complete contrast to the young boy's mood. Once over the bridge, Tommy began to think seriously as to where he could possibly have lost his post office book. His spirits sank lower and lower. Then, just as he passed the post office he saw a big notice up it read 'Post Office savings book found'. Tommy's hopes rose up momentarily, only to be dashed once again. The post office was closed! What was he to do? He knocked but the response was as silent and as hollow as the grave.

There was little use in going home. The whole idea was to keep it a secret from his parents until he got it. And besides they would berate him for loosing so much money. Just then, a woman turned in by Creagh Lane 'What's wrong little boy?' she queried. When Tommy told her she said, "Sure, they're all gone to town, even post office people have to do their Christmas shopping too, you know." The young boy went back over the bridge. The soft, white snow, which had now thickened, fell on his slim young shoulders and covered his mop of curly black hair like a fluffy white hat. Tommy stalled by the water trough at Bank Place. In his innocence he thought that maybe he'd waylay the post office man or woman on their way back from town and ask them for his money, for he felt certain that it was his savings book. As he sat, sadly musing by the water trough, he heard Cannock's ring out six loud, resonant gongs. In disbelieving manner, he glanced across at the beautiful old Custom house clock. Yes, he agreed reluctantly, as his heart sank deeply, it is six o' clock. Frantically, he ran up Rutland Street and stopped outside 'Poll Carr's' shop. The soft, fresh snow suddenly turned to muck as his eyes fell on the vacant spot. His precious gun was gone! She had sold it. He'd never forgive her, never, as long as he lived.

Wearily, he trudged home. People may have been about, but on this particular occasion this young boy saw no one. His mind was firmly locked in thoughts of that silvery, shining gun and holster. When he reached home he had his tea. "Before you go to bed Tommy" his mother said "Go over to Tracey's and collect the packet and tripe, we don't want to go hungry after midnight mass tonight and don't forget the plate of trotters. The name is on the plate, Joe knows, tell him you're Thomas Small's son." In zombie-like manner Tommy walked across the road to Tracey's.

There was a huge queue and it didn't help that he had to wait.

He was the only one for Santa to visit that night in his house, so despondently he climbed up the wooden stairs to the attic at nine-o clock. Tears wet his pillow as he dozed off, more out of weariness than anything else. Before he knew it, morning had dawned. He could hear the fry sizzling below and the delicious smell of the rashers and eggs reached his nostrils, giving him a pleasant feeling. He rubbed his eyes. Through half closed eyes he spied something shiny at the end of the bed. He blinked his eyes in utter disbelief. Could it possibly be? Yes it was his silvery shining gun and holster too! Quick as a flash he shot out of bed and took little or no time to dress in his new fairisle jumper and short corduroy pants. As he bent over to tie his shoelaces, the thought just occurred to him he now was the proud possessor of his much-admired gun and holster and after Christmas he had the huge sum of two shillings to start the New Year. So, what had promised to be a dismal Christmas had turned out to be the happiest one of his young life so far.

The Cathedral Ghost

It was the month of November. The time was four o'clock in the morning. The year was nineteen hundred and forty-eight and so far the overnight hard frost had left a hard, white carpet on the well-kept grass beneath the towering twelfth century Cathedral of St. Mary's in the ancient city of Limerick. Ernest Constable shook himself awake upon hearing his old alarm bellowing its head off on the old bureau beside his bed. "Oh, Christ!' he expleted " Sure, I've hardly slept at all and its time to get up again." Reluctantly, Ernie, as he was known to all around, threw his bony, varicose veined legs on to the cold floor. "It's at times like this," he said to himself "that I almost wish I had remained with the farming out in Adare." Ernest Constable, together with his wife Francesca, son Rodney and daughter Heather had almost two decades ago moved from the country upon securing his job as caretaker of St Mary's Cathedral, By nature Ernie was a nomad and never stayed anywhere long enough to take root. Lucky for him his wife Francesca was of a placid nature and readily went along with whatever he decided to do. So far, he had richly enjoyed his job as caretaker of the Cathedral and grounds and was looking forward to many more years.

Nothing had ever happened to make him think otherwise that was until this very morning. He pulled up his pants and secured his braces firmly over both shoulders, then sat on the bed again to put on his black leather boots. Normally he would have tapped on Rodney's door before descending the stairs. On this particular morning however, he decided to let him sleep on as he had helped the previous day to dig a grave which was to house the remains of the wife of Col. Andrew George Lefroy on the following Monday. He had predeceased her by ten years. As he carefully plod his way down the stairs the fine old Stewart clock in the parlour rang out the hour one, two, three, four solid gongs. The following day was Sunday and the lofty old Cathedral would have to be heated in good time for the first service. It was Ernie's job on the eve of any service to see that the fire in the old furnace was lit and kept stoked with coke throughout the early hours of the morning.

Ernie Constable made his way through the choir room, down the hall and in to the Cathedral. It was dark, very dark. Even the magnificent stained-glass windows failed to admit the slightest bit of light, for outside, darkness hung like a pall all over the sleeping city. He knew every square foot of the Cathedral and therefore never found it necessary to bring along a lamp to light his way. Just as he was about to descend the two stone steps leading to the door which would eventually lead him to the furnace room, he heard a noise. It appeared to come from the West Door. Hesitantly he side- glanced in its direction but saw nothing. Then five seconds later it came again, this time a bit stronger, more persistent. Although he had awoken only ten minutes previous, he certainly had all his senses about him .He tried to tell himself it was the wind but there was no wind that night. It was frosty, crisp and biting cold, all the more reason thought the old sexton to get that furnace on as quickly as possible. Just as he attempted to open the door leading to the cobblestones, he was again stopped in his tracks for it was for the third time in the space of sixty seconds that he heard the loud noise coming from the direction of the West Door. Only this time the banging was even more persistent than the previous two times. A very definite thumping it was, as if someone urgently wished to gain entry. The poor old sexton was rooted to the spot where he stood. He wondered what he should do .Oh, he thought if only Rodney were here, he'd know what to do but there was absolutely no way he could retrace his steps. He must think for himself and act quickly. The furnace had to be lit no matter what else. Then the banging got louder and louder. Ernie became increasingly frightened. A cold sweat betook his normally calm, composed demeanour. Then suddenly as if driven by some force outside himself, Ernie slowly walked past the little chapel where a stupendous marble statue to Henry, Lord Glentworth, lay prone. So many times he had observed that same marble statue over the years. Tonight however, it took on an altogether sinister appearance. The white marble portrayed a ghost-like whiteness. Slowly, very slowly he made his way past the little doorway, beyond which stood the spiralling stone staircase leading to the Cathedral Tower. The banging subsided. "Thank God!" But brief, all too brief was the interlude. For, as he hesitantly turned to go back his steps were instantly arrested by the re-occurrence of the unrelenting banging once again. Only this time he seemed to be drawn to the spot from whence the urgent banging was coming from. He knew not from where he got the strength to keep going, for by now his two knees felt like lumps of jelly. " Knock, Knock, Knock," came the sound steadily, persistently. Somehow it seemed to urgently evoke a reply. He was now but one yard from the famed West Door of the ancient cathedral. His face bore a death-like pallor beneath a fine thick crop of sage like, snow-white hair. His heart thumped, thumped, thumped. So loudly it thumped that he thought at one stage that it might fly out of his body altogether. "Oh," he breathed once again "If only Rodney were here, he might be able to go outside and see what's banging so urgently at this ungodly hour. Now as he stood by the West door, he wondered should he open it, for the banging had stopped. Then just as he returned the large bunch of keys to his pocket, he was once again shaken out of his very wits. "Bang, Bang" came the incessant, urgent sound reverberating around the vast stone hollow edifice. His right hand shook as he reached for his bunch of keys for the second time at that very moment as if to accentuate the eeriness of the situation, a hound bayed. So loudly it bayed. Hauntingly, the echo remained long after the baying had stopped Then, for one brief second, silence prevailed, no banging no baying. Ernie thought he saw a ball of white light fly all around, At one stage it seemed to reach highest point of the lofty building. The poor old sexton was in such a state of shock that he found it difficult to differentiate fantasy from reality. Finally, he managed very shakily to place the key in the lock of the West Door. Cagily, he ventured to open one side. Fear of the unknown played havoc on his normally calm and peaceful mental state. What would he find upon opening the big black door? What manner of being would one encounter? Possibly a strange sort of being? For only such could have evoked this unnatural fear in poor Ernie as he went about his normal chore. When he opened the big black door, however, much to his surprise and dubious relief the now much shaken Sexton found no one at all in any way shape or form .He ventured outside and descended the ten stone steps outside the West Door "Thank God !" breathed Ernie to himself "Thank God" He then descended the final four steps leading to the cemetery proper.No sign of anyone could he see? Tentatively, he glanced to the right and then to the left but no sight of anyone could he see. He walked back up the steps and as he closed the West Door he mumbled to himself "I know I wasn't hearing things, I'm sure I wasn't hearing things."

Although still very shaken by this frightening episode, he managed eventually to make his way out the side door and on to the close-knit cobblestones. In his present trembling state, he hardly noticed the 18th Century Sexton Vault or its close neighbour The Barrington Vault with its distinctive church-like door bearing four air holes. Ponderously he ascended the four high steps leading to the furnace room having passed the Barrington's Vault. Never before had he worked so deftly and so swiftly in setting the fire alight. For he was conscious of having wasted possibly an hour in the Cathedral. To is utter dismay, he was later to learn that the entire episode took only about three minutes. He exited from the furnace room descended the four high steps and re-entered the Cathedral. Equipped with more courage than good sense, he made his way through the choir room and back to his house, which stood adjacent to the Cathedral. The old clock registered half past four as he made his way upstairs to bed. Normally he would have re-set his clock for six when he would again rise to stoke the fire in the furnace room. However, on this particular occasion he felt there was no need for that. He would definitely not be sleeping!

Sombre darkness had just been replaced by a chirpy dawn when Ernie again crept stealthily down his stairs unbeknown to the family. The old clock in the kitchen struck out six bells. This time when he reached the Cathedral's interior he was greeted by a semblance of light that was gently admitted by means of the magnificent multi-coloured stained glass windows. He made his way to the furnace room. It was a far different scene now than two hours previous. After stoking the fire he again returned to the Cathedral to make ready for the eight-o clock service. Then, as if to fill in time before his breakfast he decided to go and check on the grave that he and Rodney had dug the previous day. A day which now seemed to him like a century ago. He wanted to make sure that none of the grave had fallen in. It wouldn't look good for him if everything wasn't in ship-shape order when the undertakers arrived to check on proceedings. As he approached the six foot cavity all seemed to be in order.

People were beginning to arrive for the early morning service, some in cars more on foot, Then as the sexton casually moved forward to peer into the grave he all but lost his set of false teeth down the six foot drop. For there, in all its pristine glory at the bottom of the grave lay an army uniform, highly bedecked with various stripes of honour. Heavy medals proudly hung from out of both breast pockets. Full length it lay there as if on someone. There was, however, no human or body in sight. Quick as lightning the poor old sexton retreated. "Oh be the Christ!" he wailed " That must have been the ghost of old Col. Lefroy knocking at the West Door during the night." As soon as the eight o clock service began, Ernie made a quick getaway through the choir room and into his house where he joined his wife and son for breakfast. "Do ye know what?" he blurted out as he sat down " No father what?" asked Rodney. "If my straight hair didn't nearly curl last night it never will" he began. "Why, what happened?" asked Francesca. He began by telling them that the ghost of Co. Lefroy was knocking frantically at the West Door during the night. I suppose, remarked his wife good humouredly I suppose he was anxious to get Isabella out of the Cathedral as quickly as possible. Well sighed the old sexton he might have the good grace to wait until daylight. Frightened the life out of me so he did the old scoundrel." "Aw give the poor chap a chance, Father" chimed in Rodney. Don't you know that ghosts only stalk the night?" Then pouring him another mug of hot tea, Francesca said "Get that inside you, twill do you the world of good. "And if you don't believe me," he said to Rodney, "You can come with me to the grave afterwards and there you'll see Lefroy's uniform in almost all its glory." "Alright I'll do that," laughed Rodney, winking at his mother.

After breakfast Rodney accompanied his father to the grave of Col. Andrew George Lefroy. As if to dispel the obvious seriousness of the situation, Rodney lit up his "Sweet Afton." He even managed to whistle a tune. "You wont be whistling in another minute, me boy, I can tell you," cautioned his father. Rodney was first to approach the grave in lighthearted manner. "See father," he began while peering into the grave "Noth.....ing "Oh be Jesus!" he wailed drawing back. 'What is it Rodney, didn't I prepare you well for the situation?" "Not for this father , you didn't. You never said that Lefroy was in uniform." "But he wasn't" assured his father "Well he's there now wailed Rodney emphatically. Ernie walked confidently over and peered into the grave. Instantly he drew back, so shocked was he upon sighting of the body of old Lefroy enclosed in an army uniform. The following day at precisely two o'clock the funeral of Isabella Lefroy took place. Of course, they had to cover old Lefroy earlier that day. Everything was in ship-shape order when the Undertaker arrived looking the very essence of undertakerability in his black bowler hat, black kid gloves and shoes so shiny that Rodney thought he mustn't have a spit that was ever known left in his mouth. Ernie was never so glad to have done with any funeral in his whole life. As he shovelled the last morsel of earth atop the well-formed mound he breathed "Thank God the ould scoundrel has her at last." Later that day the much-respected sexton found out that old Lefroy was a great man for the hounds during his lifetime.

Masie

Let's imagine for a while that we are back in the 1920's. Around that time, there lived on a stretch of road between Liscannor and Lisdoonvarna an old lady called Masie. Masie was known for her kindness to all during her earlier years.. With her black-shawl and a full-length dress, that seemed to be constantly covered by a spanking white cotton apron. She was now the typical ageing lady of that period. For, if Masie wasn't dusting every piece of delf in her dresser, then she was ironing the white linen sheets with the old iron, which she kept heated on the hob. But everybody knew, that Masie's pride was her brown bread and her white soda bread. The neighbours often said, "Sure you could say five decades and the Hail Holy Queen while Masie was kneading her dough!". And that was the greatest tribute Masie could receive, for didn't her mother before her always say, " If you knead well, in the bread 'twill tell."

For some strange reason, Masie never married, although she was known to tell of a few interested parties. There was Bill Gantley, a fine looking, broad shouldered man with dark deep set eyes. The very look of him would put any woman's heart aflutter. Bill was a well to do pig-buyer, and on his way home from the fairs he was known to stop for a mug of tea and griddle cake at Masie's. The story goes that Bill got tired of waiting and at the first opportunity he emigrated to America.

Then there was Frank Watts, Oh, a bright one he was in every way. The neighbours for miles around would go to Frank if they had any problems to be sorted out. They used to say he had the wisdom of Solomn. Now Frank it seems fancied Masie more than the other way round. One might have thought that Masie held herself somewhat aloof. She resembled for all the world, the Purdons of Limerick so long ago; who resided on the old Baal's Bridge, and who thought no man was good enough for them. Anyway, Frank had no luck with Masie, so one September he took off to Lisdoonvarna where he met his future wife Katie.

Now there was one more spark in Masie's past and that was Charlie Hobbins. Ah!. There was a man for you, hard working, a fine build, resolute mouth and firm chin, denoting character. He was known as the man to outdo all others in making a proper stack of hay. They came from near and far with their ponies and asses to be shod, for it was known that Charlie Hobbins had the gentlest touch with animals. In short, Charlie was a most genial man. Rumour had it, but this was merely pure speculation, that he was left a good legacy many years before. However, what many did not know was that Charlie Hobbins had a weak heart, which he never gave in to. His philosophy being "I'll work until the Lord calls me". Sad to relate, Charlie passed away in his fifty-fourth year, just when he would have been at a good marriageable age. Masie was so heartbroken, she couldn't attend the funeral. Instead she remained at home that afternoon and baked four cakes of bread, kneading, kneading for over an hour trying to forget. As the earth cloaked poor Charlie's remains a door closed forever across Masie's heart.

That was all in the past. Masie was now seventy-five. She still baked, was friendly to all, but of the many topics Masie discussed, she never referred to her financial affairs. In fact, around this time the neighbours were beginning to feel sorry for Masie.

One day as she went to the back for a few bits of turf for the fire, she had a fall which rendered her slightly incapacitated for many a year. Each of the neighbours in turn took on her various tasks. One would bake, another would dust all the delf in the dresser, while yet another washed and ironed. Sam Shorten, another good neighbour tended to Florrie the cow and the many fowl, that Masie kept.

As time went on, Daniel Dodge, the doctor, came all the way from Lisdoonvarna once a month to visit Masie. As well as the trouble caused by the fall, she now suffered from a weakening of the heart and lungs. This kind, caring man would never accept one brown penny from Masie nor did she press him to accept either. This state of affairs went on for a good many years, everyone offering their services but no one complaining, "Wisha poor 'oul Masie", they'd say "One day we might be old and infirm and poor, God knows."

It was on the eve of our Saviours birth in the year 1930 that Masie passed away peacefully. All the neighbours waked her and even Daniel Dodge came from Lisdoonvarna for the burial. Fr. John Holman, in his eulogy, recounted what a fine upstanding lady, Masie was, how she bore her sufferings bravely and he continued, "Even though she wasn't blessed with a semblance of riches, she never seemed to mind. She was blessed with serenity and never lost that glint in her eye" then he finished by saying "I feel my good people that at this very moment, Masie is smiling down on all of us" How true!

In the ensuing weeks, as if by some innate instinct, the neighbours continued to go to poor old Masie's house. Whether it was out of respect or what, none could tell, but this they did know, they wanted to keep that little house alive. They continued to bake, dust, light the fire and tend to the cattle and fowl. They seemed to be acting in anticipation of some great event. No one said very much but each in their own way had a most unusual feeling.

About six weeks later, as spring was about to cast its magical spell on the quiet, dull village, an unusual horse-drawn carriage was observed arriving. Several pairs of eyes peered from the lace-curtained windows at various vantage points A tall, distinguished-looking man of around sixty emerged from the carriage, carrying a case in his hand. He was observed to be enquiring from children playing. "Now who was he?" wondered the inquisitive eyes behind the curtains and "and what does he want?" Then Madge Ward was startled by her young daughter's voice, "Mama, Mama, there's a man out there and he wants to know where Masie lived. He said has she anyone left. He's very nice." "Oh will you whist up child, " said Madge "and don't be havin' so much talk!" Then swift as a gazelle Madge left the house, closed the door, and placed the key in her apron pocket leaving the young girl inside. Once outside Madge swiftly scurried to her nearest neighbour Kitty and related what she had just heard. "Well Kitty" said she excitedly "What do you think? Had Masie any relatives or what? Someone will have to talk to the man". "Go on Kitty" she urged "You go first, you do the talking for you have most of your teeth and he'll understand you better."

So out the door went Kitty, closely and very inquisitively followed by Madge. 'Ah may God bless you Sir, isn't it great the Spring is upon us again." "Good day my good ladies" replied the well-dressed gent, doffing his hat at the same time. "I understand one of your neighbours died last Christmas" he said, "May I be shown to her house please?" The women, still wondering but saying nothing, accompanied the gentleman to Masie's dwelling, which they were very happy to admit that they had kept alive. As they approached the threshold, the homely aroma of the recently baked griddlecakes coupled with the smell of the turf fire gave the gentlemen a great sense of warmth. "Now" he said as he entered "Who is Masie's next of kin?" The two women advised the gentleman whom they now knew to be Clement Grant that Masie to be sure had no relations at all. "Well" said Mr Grant "I am the bearer of very important matters, could you get the parish priest here and maybe the doctor too." The women told him that while they could easily get the priest within half an hour, it could take until after the Angelus to fetch the doctor. Clement Grant agreed that he would wait, for he had a matter of great importance to disclose to the entire village. As you can well imagine a great amount of fussing ensued. There was little bother experienced in contacting the parish priest, but the good doctor, well that was an entirely different matter. As luck would have it, the carriage that had transported Clement Grant to his destination had a delivery to make in Lisdoonvarna so he was able to pick up the doctor.

As Dr. Dodge entered Masie's old dwelling, he no more than the neighbours now gathered there, knew what was about to follow. By now, however, things had become somewhat clearer. They knew that the latest visitor to their village was a man of law, a solicitor some whispered "Oh, May God be praised " they sighed "What's going to happen?" As silence descended on Masie's cottage, Clement Grant began to speak "My good people, Reverend Father and Revered Doctor, I arrived here today with the anticipation of finding some far out relation of one Masie Slattery. It has come to my notice" he continued "that no such relation exists" By now you could hear a pin drop, those who wished to sneeze didn't dare for fear of breaking the spell. As the door was closed, children could be seen straining on their tippy toes in an effort to get a glimpse of what was going on inside. "Now" continued Mr. Grant "I wont keep you in suspense any longer, Masie Josephine Slattery has left the sum of

£890.2shillings and six pence." Well, there was one concerted gasp! Then, "Imagine that, would you ever think, wasn't she deep?" and so on. "As it transpires" continued Mr Grant " If Miss Slattery does not have any relatives it is my duty to see to it that the said amount is divided equally among the fifteen households in the village as well as the good Doctor, who I understand, tended to Miss Slattery free during her final years". Disbelief was etched on Dr Dodge's face most of all, for he had travelled many a rough road to tend to "poor" old Masie.

Before leaving, the solicitor enquired whether they wished to ask any question. "Yes" braved one "How did Masie come by all that money?" It seems that when Charlie Hobbins died at the age of fifty-four, he left a large amount to Masie, thus proving how much he loved her. Masie, unbeknown to anyone, had banked the money. Since that being many years ago, the money grew and grew since then. And as the money grew, Masie's regard for her good neighbours likewise grew and rather than whittle it to one or two, she left it so everyone got a share. It would then appear that, Masie died as she had lived, everyone's friend.

Romance at 'The Mary Rose'

Madge descended the steps of the Augustinian Church. She felt secure having attended her daily Mass, a good start to the day, she always assured herself. Since her husband's death, two years previously, she had made it a practise to walk into town every morning to attend Mass. Madge was in her early fifties and having reared two in family who had emigrated to Australia, as well as being through the trauma of a terminally ill partner for two years before his demise, she was just recently beginning to find herself again. In short, Madge was becoming a person in her own right. She spent most mornings after Mass in and about town. Occasionally she would visit the library and secure a few Mills and Boone romances for evening reading. Since her husband's death, she didn't socialise too much as she felt somewhat out of place as all her friends went out with their husbands or partners. Madge kept fit by walking daily in and out of town. She possessed handsome, dark good looks and a friendly and accessible personality was most certainly her forte.

Madge crossed Limerick's busiest street and spent a few romantic minutes daydreaming in front of the window of O'Mahony's' Bookshop, which for the festive season had taken on a magical winter wonderland look. She held her basket crooked in her elbow and snug against her as if allowing herself the security of a close friend. As it was just two weeks before Christmas, and she was on the look out for a present or two, she decided to go down to Roches Stores to browse. She always found this store most amenable, especially since the off-licence allowed her the pleasure of a discreet purchase of a naggin of whisky or brandy weekly. 'Hello Madge,' someone greeted, 'You're looking great'. It as a former workmate of Madge's when they shared a sewing machine line in then thriving Danus clothes factory twenty years before. 'Oh hello Lilly' greeted Madge 'How's yourself? We won't feel now until Christmas' 'Oh yea' replied Lilly 'I'm having an amount of visitors, I don't know how I'll get over it.' Well, thought Madge 'I wish I had your trouble'. Even though Madge was one of the friendliest people, her immediate relatives were limited and for the past two Christmases had spent the entire festive season very much alone.

She purchased a few presents and crossed diagonally to the other side of the street, She normally headed up to 'Finn's' for mid-morning coffee but the recently opened 'Mary Rose Restaurant' in 'Todd's' big department store was causing quite a buzz, so Madge decided to give it a try. 'Sure' she said to herself 'Isn't my time my own.' Madge collected her tray and slid it along the rails. The food was so attractively presented that it proved a major temptation to Madge. She ordered orange juice, a small pot of coffee, and a Danish pastry, which she requested to be heated. Although it was her first encounter with the 'Mary Rose', Madge found the staff exceptionally friendly and had already promised herself a return visit any morning she happened to be in town. She glanced around the crowded restaurant and spotted a lovely little table for one. She lay her basket down beside it and then returned for her tray. Somehow as she sat down, she had a marvellous feeling of well being, as if good fortune was about to befall her in one form or another. She unbuttoned her coat and allowed it to hang loosely about her legs. She then rescued 'The Irish Independent' from her shopping basket and absent-mindedly glanced at the main headlines. Then, suddenly, without warning, she was rivetted to the spot. Over the rim of her glasses she saw a rather tall gentleman with very fine features. He was waiting there patiently in line to be served. He seemed to stand out from the crowd. He was totally unlike any other man she had ever seen in the city before. Even from a distance, his fine large dark eyes bespoke a contented disposition. Madge cleared her throat and made an abortive effort to tidy her streaming coat. She instantly began to feel uneasy and for the life of her she couldn't tell why.

She sipped her coffee, forgetting to add any milk and almost burned her tongue. By this time she was quite embarrassed by her own unexplainable frustration. She, solid old Madge, the mistress of her owns emotions, becoming flustered at the sight for a mere man! But this was no mere man. His bearing gave all the evidence of a well-bred gentleman, possibly even of aristocratic stock. And judging from his clothes he would appear to belong to the equestrian way of life. A maverick of a man, thought Madge. Madge continued reading the headlines that had now become a blur. She pickled her coffee with salt, and made herself drink it for appearances sake. From her side eye she noticed the gentleman seat himself at another table for one directly across from her. He removed his overcoat, gloves and cap revealing a crop of dark well-groomed hair with greying sideburns, giving an added maturity to this already excellent man. Without a doubt he was impeccable. He removed a copy of 'The Irish Times' from the inside pocket of his overcoat and began to page through it while he waited for his tea to cool down. As he read one particular article intently, Madge had the advantage of observing him at her leisure. Then it happened, he stopped reading, politely removed the spoon from his cup, and began to take a sip. In so doing, he glanced over and caught Madge looking straight at him. For one split second it seemed as if time stood still. Two people who up to this time were completely unaware of each other's existence appeared to be transfixed in a gaze of disbelief. When the spell regressed to normality, Madge stood up to go, picked up her wicker shopping basket and placing her newspaper in it. As she passed his table he smiled warmly and Madge reddened. Once outside she breathed a sight of relief. What was it about this man that made me feel so uneasy, she thought. As she emerged out on to the William Street exit, Madge seemed to move with an added spring in her step, like one in the clouds, divorced from the harsh reality of this world. When she arrived home, she immediately lit her open fire, relieved herself of her high heels and slid into a comfortable pair of slippers. She opened her naggin of whiskey and topped the glass up several times. She stretched out on the couch and sipped for about an hour in a semi-daze. Before she knew it, the bottle was nearly empty. By this time she was about to fall into a deep peaceful sleep.

The next few days were busy ones for Madge and she hardly gave a second thought to the incident at 'The Mary Rose'. She decided to buy a medium sized boneless stuffed duck for Christmas. Being stubbornly independent by nature, she preferred not to encroach on the various relatives she had in and around the city. For the past two years, she had diplomatically declined every well meant offer by them to have Christmas dinner at their place. On the Tuesday before Christmas, Madge went into town to purchase her boneless stuffed duck at Noel O'Connor's in Wickham Street. Hadn't she heard the voice of 'John The Man' for the past months shouting over the local airwaves 'Go on go up to 'The Happy Butcher', sure who'd be hungry!' So Madge thought 'well I suppose I could do worse'. She skipped off briskly on that cold frosty morning air clutching her wicker basket in the crook of her elbow. After her purchase she made her way down William Street. The sky had just expelled soft flutter of snow and the city began to take on an almost magical appearance. On the way down the street Madge received several good will festive greetings. By the time she reached the side entrance to 'Todd's', Madge's smart red, fur collared coat had taken on a snowman-like appearance. It was with a great sense of relief that she made her way up to 'The Mary Rose'. Having made her purchase she found herself a table for two as all the single tables were occupied. Madge composed herself and sampled a large chunk of Black Forest and was just about to eat another slice when she was interrupted between fork and mouth by the very cultured voice of a gentleman. 'May I have the pleasure of joining you at this table madam?'. Raising her eyes, Madge was frozen to the spot on seeing that the voice was that of the selfsame gentlemen she had seen the previous week. Naturally she was nervous for a moment or two, but she politely acquiesced without hesitation. He placed his snow-flaked umbrella under the table as he removed his cap and coat. He was the first to break the ice; "Didn't I see you here last week?'. Within a few minutes, Madge learned that the name of this rather refined equestrian type gentleman was Clarence Dante who lived in a ranch- type house out in the picturesque village of Adare. He was a little over sixty and a former army colonel who had taken early retirement. Oh, thought Madge I wish the ground would open up and swallow me, how am I going to be able to converse with this fellow?. But these negative thoughts proved vain, for Clarence turned out to be the most reassuring man she had met in years. He was a most interesting conversationalist who was conscious only of the person he was talking to. Madge and Clarence chatted away as if they had known each other all their lives. They seemed wrapped up in each other's conversation and seemed totally oblivious to anyone else around. That morning in particular, Madge's coffee break lasted all of one hour. One thing she had summed up, Clarence Dante had a quiet, yet rich personality .He was sincere she thought, and perhaps a little lonely. Before parting they made a pact to meet every Friday at 'The Mary Rose'. Madge let him have her telephone number.

Christmas came and went. Madge seemed to experience a new lease of life, remaining ever conscious of her very distinguished recent acquaintance. After her husband's death, she would never have imagined something like this happening. But life sometimes has a habit of challenging you, staring you in the face and saying 'Come on life is there for living, give of yourself, what's left of it anyway. Go on make someone happy'. For Madge the New Year dawned with an invigorating enthusiasm. She looked forward to Fridays and her meetings with Clarence at 'The Mary Rose'. For Clarence, meeting Madge on Fridays was his salvation and he also seemed to experience a new lease of life. As the harshness of Winter gave way to the mildness of Spring and spring eventually relented to the beauty of Summer, Madge and Clarence grew to be fond friends. By this time they both knew each other's birth date and remembered it too. All the while the staff at 'The Mary Rose' were becoming intrigued by this budding romance. They really looked forward to Fridays. Behind the scenes they joked "Wonder when the big day will be?" Secretly the head lady Freda had quite an eye for Clarence. But Clarence had eyes for Madge alone. Clarence was the prototype of a man who was every middle-aged woman's dream; courteous, demure; with almost intoxicating, dashing dark good looks and above all he bore every appearance of being extremely wealthy. What Freda did not know was that outside of their weekly meetings at 'The Mary Rose', Clarence and Madge went on many outings to Kilkee. There they frequently dined in 'Manuels' an exclusive and romantic seafood restaurant situated on the road to Corbally, a quaint old village outside Kilkee.

Before driving to 'Manuels' they would sit for almost an hour in Clarence's car. They would dream romantically while observing the red sun set after its tiresome day spent shining over Kilkee's vast expansive bay. They enjoyed many happy weekends in the safe clutches of 'Limerick's Riviera.' Madge was simply swept off her feet.

Summer gave way to Autumn, and by November the city had again become abuzz with anticipated festive excitement. Clarence and Madge continued their weekly meetings at 'The Mary Rose' and what is more they lived for each other's company. Before they knew it Christmas was again approaching and they each anticipated possible gifts for one another. Clarence had no hesitation at all. He would give Madge a gold watch with her name engraved on it. He would purchase it from the most renowned jeweller in the city 'Irwin's' in Patrick Street, that most distinctive black painted shop with rich gold lettering. Madge wondered what do you give to a man who has everything? Then she decided "Sure you can't go wrong with the old pair of slippers. He might remember me while wearing them relaxing by the warm fire as he sips his Benedictine and puffs on his pipe out on his ranch in Adare."

By Christmas week Madge was all prepared. It was the Friday before Christmas. All was in readiness. She had her package and her card. It was with the excitement of a teenager in love that she anticipated her meeting with Clarence. She entered the restaurant and went over to what had now become their regular table. She awaited Clarence's arrival before ordering. Fifteen minutes went by and no sign of Clarence. Thirty minutes elapsed and still no sign of Clarence, what could be wrong she wondered. 'Maybe his car gave trouble'. There was a particularly hard frost the previous night. She read and reread the newspaper. She was conscious of the staff observing her. 'Must be all off' quipped Freda. Then as if waking from a bad dream a rather-loud voiced woman rasped, "I suppose you're Madge." Poor Madge looked up pathetically "Why yes and may I ask who are you?" "I'm Sybil Dante, I believe you're very well acquainted with my husband Clarence" she replied proudly. It's a good thing Madge was in a sitting position, for her knees had suddenly turned to jelly as she looked at her verbal assailant in disbelief. "Oh,' continued Sybil stingingly. 'Just as I thought, you didn't even know of my very existence. Because Clarence didn't mention his having a wife you foolishly believed he had none. How utterly childish of you.'. By this time, Sybil, a woman of almost seventy years had sat down on the edge of the chair opposite Madge .She went about removing her sleek, long, black gloves with all the verve of a seasoned seductress, eyeing Madge with evil intent all the while. The removal of her gloves served to reveal a sizeable amount of real gold, between rings and bracelets. Despite her age Sybil Dante bore the appearance of a woman ten years younger. She was tall and elegant and carried herself in such a manner, that made others feel she had the world at her command. Her very fine looks, however were cancelled by the fact that she possessed a spiteful, vindictive and churlish nature. She had already seen two husbands down and had gained well financially from both. Poor Clarence, to put it politely fell a victim of her charms ten years ago. In that particular year she was introduced to him at an annual Hunt Ball. From the moment she set eyes on him, she lost no ground in getting her female talons into this quiet, reserved, well-bred man. In actual fact she never lost track of his movements from that first meeting. That was until the months previous to this meeting with Madge. As she prepared her husband's suits for the cleaners she came across a tiny piece of paper with writing on it in one of his lesser used suits. Under the name, Madge, in just about decipherable writing were the words 'Every Friday morning at 'The Mary Rose." So she thought suspiciously, when she came across this totally unexpected piece of information, can you ever be up to the men? I'll see to it that this nice, cosy liaison is split into smithereens. Pretending nothing to Clarence, she arranged by deceit that he was elsewhere in this particular Friday. Sybil made absolutely sure in any case that he was far away from Limerick.

Poor Madge sat perplexed in front of her half cold cup of coffee and the untouched croissant that one of the staff had supplied to her in a gesture of comradeship. Having observed the episode with disbelief, although completely taken unawares by this bombshell disclosure, for some odd reason, her concern and sympathies lay completely with Clarence. In all her years she had never come across a woman with such a dominating and positively hurtful personality. By this time of course, the attractive elderly lady had stormed out of the restaurant, with lengthy coat swishing as she manoeuvred her way in a most unladylike manner through the occupied tables. The lady from Adare had most certainly left her mark on 'The Mary Rose'. Those at the nearby tables couldn't help but hear the rasping voice as she reproached poor, defenceless Madge. She definitely had succeeded in intimidating her husband's friend. Madge exited quietly, leaving in her wake a number of pairs of pitiful, inquisitive and wondering eyes. Once outside, the frost but helped to accentuate her already bleak numbed feelings. Although she hadn't smoked in five years, she now longed for a smoke. She bought a packet of twenty in a small shop in Little Catherine Street and made her way, somewhat in a daze up to 'Tom Collins" Pub. When Ted was alive, they used to go there every week for a quiet drink. They loved the pictures of Old Limerick that augmented the already quaint ambience. As she slowly plodded up Catherine Street towards Cecil Street, Madge thought well they serve coffee, maybe if I slip in for a drink it won't be noticed. She ordered a double brandy and found herself a quiet secluded spot at the back. There she plonked herself down in a state of abject desperation and with a terrible feeling of dejection.

Before taking her first sip, she lit up a cigarette. Her thoughts automatically drifted back to her first encounter with Clarence Dante. Now at this moment in time, the entire affair seemed to fade sadly into oblivion. It was as if a smokescreen had been drawn over the past year or more. Why didn't he tell me, she thought again and again, why? The thing that bothered her most of all was the fact that, how a fine refined man like Clarence could be joined in matrimony to such a female battle-axe, albeit a well persevered and rather attractive one. As she sat and mused, she felt as if the bottom had fallen out of her world. Just when she was again beginning to have a full and meaningful life, it was instantly snapped from under her nose and in the cruellest manner possible. She was devastated. She wished she could sleep through Christmas As she demurely made her exit by the back door about an hour and a half later, she was very glad that semi-darkness had begun to descend. She felt awful and she thought that she possibly looked awful too. As she boarded the bus for home she almost wished it were some aeroplane about to transport her to Jamaica or some such place.

Meanwhile, Sybil Dante having successfully operated her sad, sorry bit of business, drove her silver Merc up the long and winding driveway leading to her ranch-like house. She was determined not to disclose the object of her finding or the nature of her visit to Limerick that day. The following week being Christmas week, found Clarence Dante in Limerick, where he paid his customary visit to 'The Mary Rose' .He was most concerned at not seeing any sign of his friend, Madge. When he arrived home, he telephoned but oddly enough the phone seemed to be constantly off the hook. On the second Friday after Christmas, Clarence went again to his favourite restaurant for lunch. Seeing no sign of Madge, he became somewhat puzzled. What could have gone wrong, he thought. She was in great form the last time I saw her. As weeks extended into months and as sprightly Spring gave way to golden Summer, Clarence continued to pay his weekly visit to 'The Mary Rose' in hopes of one day meeting Madge again. He was never to be the wiser of his wife's visit with Madge. Meanwhile, Madge crumbled mentally in her own little world. She had the craft to have her phone number changed. For much as she still cared deeply for Clarence, she didn't wish to have any further contact with him. Sybil had succeeded far beyond her own devious expectations in totally demolishing Madge's spirit. So, try as he might, Clarence failed to make contact with Madge, for she had her new number listed ex-directory and he failed to find her postal address. Both parties, in their own individual way was feeling an abysmal sense of loss. Theirs had been a true meeting of souls and had all the earmarks of a healthy friendship. Sybil Dante silently nurtured a marvellous sense of selfish satisfaction at having gained the upper hand of her husband, while still managing to keep him completely in the dark.

It was November the fourth and Madge sat in her tiny kitchen drooling over her second cup of coffee and as she absent-mindedly paged through the previous night's 'Limerick Chronicle,' she began to reminisce as she observed the old photos printed in 'Down Memory Lane'. Meanwhile 'John The Man' rambled on through his morning radio programme urging the dressing gown brigade to 'Get up outa dat." She heard Marianne Faithful sing 'Wrong Road Again' and "Blanket on the Ground" being sung by Philomena Begley, after which John commented " Oh that brazen hussy! Let her off with her blanket on the ground, she can't be up to any good!'. Crystal Gayle's rendition of "River Road" with its opening line of "Here I go once again with my suitcase in my hand I'm running away down River Road" heralded the News followed by the death notices read by 'John The Man' himself with many an appropriate comment thrown in. 'Bennis, Joseph better known as Jock at his residence (I wonder would he be anything to the Young Munster Bennis's?) Dante nee

Robinson of Empyrean Lodge, Adare, Co. Limerick, following an accident in Switzerland'… Madge blinked twice, consumed a large gulp of cooled down coffee and rushed over to turn up the radio and in so doing missed the remainder of the death notice. The amount that she heard had registered loud and clear. When she'd get 'The Limerick Leader' that evening all would-be revealed. As Madge sat by her warm fireside later she learned from the local newspaper that Sybil Dante had died in a coach crash as their group was being toured around Switzerland's scenic spots. She had taken a Winter break to over the long, humdrum, tedious round of common tasks that seemed to plague her everyday life of late. The body would be flown back in two days time for burial. Madge sat back, thought and pondered deeply. Poor Clarence, she wondered, how he was taking it? Her mind flashed back to that dreadful acrimonious meeting between herself and Sybil, who was then in full flight, riding her high, social horse and discounting everyone an everything that got in her way. God is just, pondered Madge, God is very just.

For the next few weeks Madge spent much of her waking hours with thoughts of Clarence, wondering how he was. Then, with the approach of Christmas, she was making herself busy again going to town. It was the Friday before Christmas week and Madge decided to make a visit to 'The Mary Rose.' She hadn't been there since that soul destroying meeting with Sybil Dante. As she held her tray, comprising of a small pot of coffee and a hot croissant she glanced around in hope of finding a suitable table for one or maybe two. Spying the back of what appeared to he her old friend Clarence, she almost dropped her tray, what should she do, she wondered? As if inspired from above, she decided instantly, I can't very well go away and I would so much like to talk to him. He sat at a table for two all by himself. .Her mind was made up, she would approach him. She came from behind and lay down her pot of coffee and hot croissant on the table 'Mind if I join you?' she queried gently. Clarence was visibly, delightfully surprised 'O, Madge' he began 'Where have you been, I've missed you so much, what happened?' He then disclosed that since their last meeting he hadn't missed even one Friday at 'The Mary Rose' in hopes of meeting her again. 'I have something to confess to you Madge' he went on. Madge felt she knew what it was and made it easy for him. She told him of his late wife's meeting with her and how terrible she felt following it. 'Oh Madge' went on Clarence 'I didn't want to tell you I was married for fear of loosing you.' He then revealed the full facts about Sybil, how she had clung to him since the very moment they had met. It wasn't until after their marriage that he sadly came to the realisation, it was his fine ranch that she was more attracted to. She insisted on having a great time always and made a rule to go for three holidays a year, preferably alone or with a female friend of her choosing. Clarence also told Madge that she had dominated him in every way since marrying

He explained how there was no way of extricating himself from this sorry situation. His happiest times were spent in simple conversation with Madge. Reading between the cracks of his conversation, it seemed to Madge that her death came as a happy release for Clarence. Madge listened attentively and offered nothing by way of reproach .She was overjoyed to have renewed their friendship once again. For she had already long given up hopes of ever seeing Clarence again and most certainly never anticipated Sibyl's early demise. About an hour later, Clarence and Madge emerged from 'Todd's' department store. As they stepped out on to O'Connell Street, a heavy fall of close-knit snowflakes obliterated Cannock's Clock, Limerick's finest old timepiece, and for decades the ideal meeting place for dating couples. Lately it had become a victim of city modernisation, rendering it much less warm looking and consequently less attractive. They shopped around for a while, after which time Clarence invited Madge home with him for the evening. Madge was only too thrilled to comply with his wishes. She could hardly believe her luck as they drove towards Adare. The roofs of the thatched cottages had taken on a magical white effect as a result of the afternoon's snow. As they drove up the golden-orange lit driveway Madge felt a marvellous sense of belonging a sense of coming home, her second home. They had an ecstatically peaceful Christmas. By the following Christmas they had married, just a few years after their first meeting at 'The Mary Rose' from whence their friendship and subsequent romance had blossomed. Clarence and Madge belonged together and were about to experience a thoroughly fulfilling life for the remainder thereof.

Autumn leaves turn gold.
Autumn years delightfully unfold.

A weird and wonderful honeymoon

Geoffrey and Judy had known each other since they were very young. They made Holy Communion together, were confirmed together, and had even learned to swim and cycle together. They were neighbours who lived in the same block of houses in Ballinasloe, Co. Galway. They had always been a carefree, happy twosome. During the great October Horse Fair each year, as they got older, they had a stand of their own to sell their wares, for Geoffrey was nimble at basket making and Judy was great at knitting. They had shared many varied experiences together, but the one I am about to relate was the strangest one they could ever remember.

A week previous to the mysterious happening, Geoffrey and Judy were married. Nothing strange about that you might say and there wasn't. Following the Church ceremony, a hooley was held at 'Ledridge's'. The celebrations went on almost into the following day, when Geoffrey and Judy left for a two-week sojourn in County Kerry. Although they were only twenty-four, they both valued the beauty that enriched every nook and corner of Ireland. And so they had decided on Kerry for their honeymoon. What is more, they used Geoffrey's old yellow Volks to take them to their destination. Geoffrey was a member of the local football club and Judy was an avid tennis player. So, on a warm sunny day towards the end of August they set off. "Just married" was sprayed all over the Volks, and tins, an old football boot, and even a tennis racquet trailing along the ground ,creating a terrible din.

The journey from Ballinasloe to Kerry although long, was a most pleasant experience for the newly weds. Having shed all the tensions normally associated with wedding preparations they both basked in the relief of their new-found freedom. Because of knowing each other for so long, they, more than the average newly weds had merely solidified an already close knit bond of many years standing. And so, they happily journeyed on taking turns at the driving.

As they entered County Kerry, the magnificent scenery that lay before their eyes took their breath away. It was akin to Paradise itself, or as they imagined this place to be. Reminiscences of "The purple heather mountain, the river running by" returned to them as they recalled the one subject they both liked at school, English, and the many joys the poetry lesson had brought to them.

After checking in to the hotel, they quickly divested themselves of their finery. Feeling much more relaxed; they went for a walk so as to loosen out their cramped bones, which were rather stiff after the long journey. So off strolled Geoffrey and Judy hand in hand, having absolutely no great illusions about the future together and therefore not likely to be disillusioned.

The following morning they rose and again dressed casually. They were out to enjoy these two weeks. A typical Irish breakfast of rashers, eggs, sausages, puddings and tomatoes was preceded by a refreshing swim. While breakfasting they decided they would got for a tour around the "Ring", relax and then return . The question was would they be able to relax after their return? The reliable old Volks started trouble free, and thundered along the winding roads, which were punctuated by several zigzag twists and turns. The old Volks manipulated these s-hook turns better than any new-born Carina. Many sleazier, flashier cars passed them out and every one without exception had an occupant or two who nodded condescendingly at them.

At one juncture of their journey, an entire family seemed to wave and nod in unison and this included the driver. All expressions without doubt seemed to say "Ah, the poor things, they'll get there eventually".

At the end of their journey they got out to relish the attributes of that famous landmark 'Kate Kearney's Cottage'. Then they took a ride in the jarvey, which they thoroughly enjoyed. Later they savoured a very fine meal. The entire afternoon was taken up with the enjoyment of these natural pleasures.

Much rejuvenated, they then sat into the old yellow Volks to return back. As Geoffrey turned the ignition on there wasn't a budge from his beloved lady whom he had christened 'Matilda' when he purchased her five years ago. She was then five years old, so now she was ten and still going strong, that was until now. "C'mon Matlida" coaxed Geoffrey as Judy sat and enjoyed his conversation with the 'other woman' in his life!. "Oh, Mother Mary help me" pleaded Geoffrey "You'd want the patience of Job with some women!" "Why don't you try the lights" interjected Judy who was always known for her practicality, "Now why didn't I think of that?" queried Geoffrey. When he went to switch on the lights he realised to his horror that the lights had been fully on for four or five hours. When getting out of the car he had stretched his hand over for the camera and had inadvertently activated the light switch.

Now, there wasn't as much as a faint glimmer. All the buses had already left and there were very few people around as semi darkness was swiftly descending. Being somewhat tired they decided to thumb a lift and sort out Matilda next morning. Wearily they waited for a at least a half an hour by the side of the road until finally a lady who was travelling in a black Morris Minor stopped and gave them a lift. They entered from either side in the back as there were a few things strewn in the middle of the back seat.

In no time at all, they were on friendly terms with the driver. She was a rather fine looking woman of around fifty-five well-built and possessing a most jovial disposition. "Of late," she told them, "My eyes have become somewhat dim, so I need to wear these glasses driving." With glasses perched on her nose and with head and chin in a permanent upward position, she looked quite the character. As she drove along she said, "He loves this stretch". They then learned that the lady's surname was Daniels. Geoffrey and Judy were beginning to think they were extremely tired for try as they might they saw no one but three of them in the car. "Oh!" continued the loquacious lady, "This will do him the world of good. We always had happy times down there." The newly weds complete and utter bewilderment was interrupted by the melodious voice of Englebert Humperdinck singing "Please Release me, Let me Go," on the radio. Then, thought Judy the practical one, "Maybe she has poor Herbie locked in the boot for some slight breach of conduct!". Remember this woman whom they now knew, as Gretta was some character. "Well Herbie" she continued "We're almost there, not so long a journey after all was it?" Geoffrey and Judy had other ideas; it was an extremely long and weird one for them. Now they mused, either your woman is slightly touched or we had poteen instead of wine but to them no man in the form of Herbie was present. If one could only have seen their individual expressions. They ranged from open mouths to terror but most of the time was just one big question mark. They thought maybe with a surname like Daniels he had gone and done a disappearing act! Because of Gretta's obvious confidence and effusive personality neither Geoffrey nor Judy thought it proper to question her on the whereabouts of her dear husband Herbie. And so, they engaged in ordinary chit chat until they reached the crossroads, which lead to their destination.

As they were both emerging from the Morris and saying "Thank you," Gretta Daniels casually said. "Would one of you kindly hand me that little wooden box there in the back seat?, You see Herbie always liked to be in the front and now that I'm about to scatter his remains where he wished them to be scattered, I'd like him beside me for the final lap of the journey." It was Geoffrey who had begun to transfer the little wooden box on Gretta's request. With the car doors firmly shut, Gretta Daniels with head tilted upwards and glasses perched on her nose continued merrily on her way with no one but Geoffrey and Judy the wiser of her font seat passenger!. The newly weds looked at each other with a look that said shall we laugh or shall we cry? They opted for the former. As they sauntered down the road to their hotel, they joked "Imagine returning from 'The Ring' with man's ashes between us?. Boy Herbie Daniels must be well shaken about by now!". Geoffrey and Judy were none the worse of their experience the following day as they made arrangements to collect 'Matlida'. On their return this time there would be nothing between them but the handbrake. They would make absolutely sure of that!

The Ingenious Curator

Ray Ryan was a most studious lad on the brink of embarking on the big bad world of business. Ray had always been the safe one at school during the late thirties. While the other lads might go on a wild spree, such as the overnight stay in the Clare Glens a few miles from the city, complete with knapsack which contained everything from a Billy can to a penknife, Ray would probably go to the old library in Pery Square. At the library which Carnegie donated in the year 1906, Ray would be frequently seen at the antique book section. He seemed, and unusual too for a lad in his late teens, to become completely engrossed in things old, whether it be books or old clocks, old furniture, art or jewellery. The chief librarian was heard to remark more than once " See that boy, he will be one of Limerick's most discerning future antique dealers"

Well, believe it or not Ray Ryan by means of delivering the 'Limerick Chronicle' each week to several outlets earned for himself just enough to get his fare to England. While there the sight of London's old curiosity shops intrigued him so much that he had a mind to overstay his planned one month sojourn. Happily he gained a tidy sum for himself through cleaning windows and polishing the exterior brass effects of the better-established businesses in London. So much for his wasteful overnight stays at the Clare Glens!. Ray knew what he wanted and was well on the way to getting there.

Three months later Ray graduated to being an antique shop's assistant. This quaint old establishment was aptly named 'Ye Olde Curiosity Shoppe.' The owner, a low sized Jewish man called Jacob, from observing Ray go in and out, thought he showed promise. Ray was thrilled with this marvellous opportunity of gaining experience in the line of business so dear to his heart. He wrote home for fear his parents would be worried and told them he was doing well and he might stay. He duly informed the folks back home that if he didn't go on these wild escapades in the Clare Glens he was hardly likely to become involved in London's undesirable side of life. And so he admonished them at home 'Don't worry' and true to his word his business was his first and last love.

Now, about this time some genuine antiques in various lines were arriving on London and Ray proved an excellent envoy for his boss, Jacob, who trusted implicitly. Ray was gifted with a sharp eye for the genuine article and Jacob appreciated this natural aptitude. As luck would have it Ray struck up a friendship with what one might call a shark in the said business. This man, ten years older than Ray, was named Roberto.

When he completed his apprenticeship as buyer for 'Ye Olde Curiosity Shoppe', Ray wished to move in ascending direction, jobwise. After the usual mechanical, plausible handshake, Jacob issued Ray with a first class reference, a reference that was to serve him in good stead for the future. In the meantime Ray Ryan decided to remain in London and wrote home to advise his parents on his decision. The time was right, the climate of antique trade rife. He and his friend Roberto, were going places very fast. By the way, Roberto was of Italian origin and was a very skilled man with his hands, The two friends decided to set up house together. They were single-minded men and both enjoyed their one passion in life, antiques.

Now one weekend, as Roberto paged through the 'London Times' his sharp eye was very much taken by a notice, which appeared in the job section. The advertisement stated 'We are looking for an enterprising young man to act as curator to our museum'. When Ray's returned, after burrowing in the many curio shops all over London, Roberto showed him the advertisement. At first glance Ray thought the job too good to be true. 'Sounds like a dream,' he remarked to his friend. Within a week Ray had posted all the necessary credentials to the said museum. A month went by before Ray received a reply to come for an interview. Ray rose particularly early on the day of the interview and set off on foot to the stated venue. When the interview was over, Ray immediately repaired to the outdoor hallway for a longed-for smoke of his pipe. He was now in the company of at least ten other hopeful interviewees. One was better than the others expounding on the year of this and the year of that as they recalled the various purchases they had made in the past were. Each interviewee in turn was told that he would be contacted one way or the other. So far so good. When each young man had expounded all his verbal expertise of antique jargon on the others the likeminded company disbanded and headed for their various destinations.

Ray and Roberto went for a drink that evening. Among other topics they discussed the possibility of Ray getting the job as curator of the museum. Roberto seemed to have an inordinate interest in his friend's future prospects. One month later when both men had almost forgotten about the museum job, a letter arrived for Ray Ryan .Opening the letter Ray read 'We are happy to inform you….' Yes, Ray would now become curator of the 'Prima Museum'. His extreme happiness was matched only by Roberto's ecstatic exuberance.

On the following Monday, Ray, dressed in smart dark suit and slim tie, set out for his new job. At home Roberto thought long and hard. One thing was sure; his inordinate interest in his friend's curatorship of the museum had more to it than first met the eye. What Ray did not know was that his friend was a superbly gifted man with his hands. The truth of the matter was, that given a picture, a piece of furniture, a medal or a book of any kind Roberto could reproduce the exact replica or at least what appeared to be the exact replica. Now with such a gift Ray's partner was nurturing very deep–seated ideas indeed. Dark they were, but oh the monetary gain, the magnificent monetary gain.

Ray returned after his first day at the museum and by his lively conversation Roberto instinctively knew that his friend was a little more than pleased. In fact, he felt that his friend had had finally found his perfect niche. As they spun their old seventy-eights classical collection that evening, Roberto seemed unduly preoccupied. Then Ray interjected 'Nice rendition of Ravel's 'Bolero' yes?'' 'Oh sorry, so sorry I was completely lost in my thoughts'. 'So I've noticed' said Ray as he puffed contentedly on his pipe, 'Anything wrong?' asked Ray, somewhat concerned for the man whose sharp intellect he had come to admire and whose easy going personality complemented his own impulsive ways. 'Well' said Roberto 'If you knew what I was contemplating you might not wish to lodge with me any longer or to even be my friend'. 'Oh come now Roberto,' said Ray, 'You know me better than that, I am absolutely shockproof. Let's hear it'.

Consuming a generous swig of whiskey, Roberto ensconced himself snugly in his armchair and after a puff or two from his old turned down pipe, he finally spilled out his thoughts. 'Ray' he said rather hurriedly 'I am expert at creating replicas.' Much relieved Ray said 'Well is that all and I thought you were contemplating murdering someone'. 'I'm not finished' said Roberto. 'Oh' said Ray 'There's more.' 'Yes much, much more' said he 'You see my good friend' he continued' I have devised a plan that could be of enormous monetary gain to us both.' 'Yes? questioned Ray, sitting a little forward in his chair in an effort to catch every word. 'Let me tell you,' said Roberto.

One hour later Ray Ryan was the recipient of some very weighty information indeed, The truth of the matter was that Roberto wished to defraud the 'Prima Museum' of its true gems. And this is how he planned to do it. Every so often Ray would bring home one item from his place of work and his partner would get very busy on creating the exact replica of that item. As soon as that was complete, work on another item would continue. And as it was yet a young museum there were hardly more than twenty or twenty-five items. What an achievement it would be to possess all those originals!

Surprisingly Ray was more than enthusiastic about this well thought out plan. He saw very little obstacles, if any, in his way. Both retired rather excited about their joint project that night. The following morning found both men equally excited. Today would be the first of many an interesting day. They could hardly contain themselves. What a brilliant prospect!

Ray, the curator, had his position well sized up. His boss and the owner of the 'Prima Museum' was as far as he could observe a most trusting individual who spent a lot of time away on antiquarian business. What Ray did not know was that Mr. Gervase Pentomy had an excessive shrewdness behind that obviously trusting veneer. In fact, even though Mr. Pentomy seemed to trust Ray Ryan with the entire running of the museum, he never failed on a certain date and at a particular time every three months, to take stock of his gems.

Completely unaware of this quarterly inventory, Ray was happy to supply Roberto with a gem from the museum every so often. The expert never failed to re-produce the exact replica, no matter what the item. Everything was going so smoothly, they could hardly believe their luck. 'Oh, Roberto, What a brain you have' said Ray one evening.' We are in line to gain a mint of money, aren't we?' 'Yes we are,' grinned his partner as he puffed contentedly on his pipe.

On the last day of June at precisely 2.15 am. Mr Gervase Pentomy donned his dressing gown and slippers and made his way downstairs to his haven of gems for his quarterly inventory. Yes, as far as he could see every item was present and in its usual position. Then, just as he was about to switch off the light and ascend the stairs, something in his mind triggered off the need for one more check. Something wasn't quite right but exactly what it was Mr. Pentomy couldn't detect. He spent two solid hours tracing and retracing his slippered footsteps around his museum. Then, just as he was about to give up, 'Eureka!' why yes, that spectacular nature picture is minus a cygnet. There was always four. It used to remind him of his quarterly inventory. Now on this particular morning, instead of four cygnets, there were only three. Though obviously concerned, Mr. Gervase Pentomy in no way grasped the full extent of his discovery.

Next day, Ray showed up for work at his usual time, whistling merrily, denoting a happy spirit. All went well that day. Visitors came, viewed the precious items, signed the open book and left. Just as Ray was about to close up, the entrance of his boss Mr.Pentomy startled him. 'Oh good day Mr. Pentomy' said Ray, 'I trust all is well'. 'Maybe and maybe not, Mr. Ryan, I have a matter that I wish to discuss with you.' Mr. Pentomy came to the point immediately. Ray put his boss's mind at ease. 'No I'm certain there was only three cygnets in the said picture' Ray replied.

When he reached home, Ray rushed into the back room. He knew that it was here that he'd find Roberto, for he was always engrossed in some type of work or other. Although all the 'Prima Museum' works were now completed. 'Roberto,' Ray blurted out 'You made a mistake we may be in grave trouble.' He then related the incident with Mr.Pentomy that day. Then, like a bolt from the blue Roberto recalled that day he was copying that Nature picture, a melee outside on the street had disturbed him. Due to that interruption, he had missed putting in the fourth cygnet. 'Oh, Ray, what shall we do?' said he. 'Don't worry yet' said Ray, 'I think I've convinced old Pentomy. However, I wouldn't be without saying a little prayer tonight, if I were you.' Ray himself was now beginning to feel very shaky indeed.

Meanwhile, back at the 'Prima Museum', Mr. Gervase Pentomy, still unconvinced, had contacted his true and trusted friend Mr. Augustus Trent. Two weeks after, when it appeared as if things had subsided. Mr. Pentomy decided to give Ryan his two-week annual break. They parted most amicably and Ray was issued with an extra £10.00 so as to 'enjoy' himself. Once Ray's back was turned, Mr.Pentomy and his old friend Augustus Trent got down to business. They spent every spare moment in the museum downstairs, investigating and resembling for all the world, Sherlock Holmes and partner. 'Tell me', queried Trent, 'How do you rate your curator, Mr Ryan,' 'Oh' retorted Pentomy, 'The best, one of the best, he's Irish you know, went to a Catholic school.' 'Is that so,' said Trent. 'Sounds almost too good to be true, if you want my opinion.' The monacled Mr. Augustus Trent moved ever so slowly about the museum observing every detail of every item. 'Pentomy' Trent suddenly called out, 'Didn't that valuable old coin have a cut edge? This one has a smooth edge.' 'What a sharp eye you have old chap,' answered the museum owner. 'Why yes of course that valuable old coin did have a cut edge. I used to love the feel of it'. It was then that both men realised that something was very, very wrong. They had a most unsavoury business to sort out and they had but two weeks to do it.

That evening, the mulled every possibility over in their minds as they pensively sipped on their whiskey. 'It must be him,' said Trent. 'No one else has access to the museum'. 'You're far too trusting' he continued, 'I always said that.' 'I'm completely baffled,' said Pentomy, shaking his head, 'What are we to do?' Trent knew exactly what to do. He was not known at all around that area. He would call on Ray Ryan's house in the guise of a clergyman, new to the town. And that was exactly what Trent did the very next day. He was not one to let the grass grow under his feet.

On the following day at twelve noon, Trent, bedecked in dark grey suit and white collar, knocked ever so gently on Ray Ryan's door. Within seconds the door opened and there before his eyes stood the object of his investigation, the much trusted curator of the 'Prima Museum.' 'Good–day my good man,'- said Trent rather plausibly, 'I'm new here and in an effort to get to know my parishioners better, I'm visiting each one, may I come in?' Even though Ray was not of this clergyman's persuasion, he did not let on. He simply answered 'Why certainly, come inside, you are most welcome.' 'Ah!' breathed the Reverend, as he as he passed the threshold. 'What an oasis for the weary traveller.' Once inside, Trent lost no time in putting all his powers of observation to good use. As Ryan went to make a pot of tea for his cultured visitor, Trent quickly detected the smell of fresh paint somewhere in the house. It told him of much renovation in a far off room. As he mused on this discovery his thoughts were interrupted by the entrance of a rather dishevelled, partly grey haired man, who had, it would seem emerged from somewhere down a hallway. 'Hello Reverend', greeted the artistic looking man, 'Ray told me you are in town, you are indeed very welcome'. Trent replied most amicably. He was struck by the worklike appearance of the man he now knew to be Roberto. As Ray returned with a pot of tea and cake, Trent could hardly believe how things were starting to piece together. 'I must be right' he thought, 'The various parts of the puzzle are beginning to fit into place.' As they bade their visitor farewell, little did they realise what had transpired in the 'clergyman's' head? Trent couldn't wait to reach Pentomy's house. 'My good friend' he blurted out while still panting, 'We've cracked it, I'm certain'. Having explained his observations, Pentomy agreed to contact the police. Early the next morning, the police arrived at the house of the two gentlemen. They had a warrant to search the house. 'For what' queried the men indignantly, 'For what?' In a short time, all would be revealed, the police promised. It didn't take the police very long to swoop upon the long room at the end of the hallway. And yes, there in all their pristine glory were the true 'Prima Museum's' gems. The look of abject consternation on the faces of Ray and Roberto told it all. The game was up and they knew it.

That evening, as a much relieved Trent and Pentomy sipped their sherry and puffed contentedly on their pipes, they marvelled at their ingenious curator and his friend, who by now were behind bars. Neither would be doing any curatoring or duplicating for a very long time. 'Well done,' said Pentomy to his good friend. 'How very astute you are.' 'From now on, I'll run the museum by myself, and by the way' he continued ' I'm giving you all the replicas. An astute man such as you should have little trouble disposing of them.' 'Quite so' laughed Trent as he proferred his glass to Pentomy for a refill. I might even succeed in passing them off for the real thing!" he added giving a knowing wink at his friend.

To find a thrifty wife

"Is that you Lionel?" called Henrietta Webster upon hearing the front door bang. "Yes, Mother" he called up the stairs, then progressed to the drawing room, muttering to himself, "Doesn't she know very well 'tis me, who else would it be?" Lionel Webster was thirty-eight. He was an only child and had lived alone with his mother for the past five years, since the sudden death of his father. They lived in what was considered to be a fashionable side of Limerick City, Victoria Terrace on the South Circular Road in a large house called "Lilac Tree". With his father's passing, Lionel had slipped snugly and conveniently into his vacant place as chief head bottle washer of the nearby Limerick Steamship Company on O'Curry Street. It was then a thriving company within sight of the majestic Shannon River where ships from all over the world arrived and docked every other week. Lionel's father, Archibald, a man of immense size, was gifted at making lucrative contracts abroad. He possessed an innate aptitude for his particular job and had a natural liking for all his fellow man and that included the "Dockers" with whom he frequently came in contact. He was in turn very well thought of by all. He smoked a turned-down pipe and was hardly ever seen without it. He had joined the shipping company as a young lad of fourteen as a messenger boy and had, by his own ingenuity, worked himself up to the much respected and responsible position, which he held until his death at the age of sixty-five.

Henrietta had been his one and only. He had fallen victim to her wiley feminine charms when but a young man of twenty-three. At a glance, she saw great monetary prospects and true to her female intuition, she had proved herself correct. From the moment she married Archibald Webster, Henrietta never experienced a poor day. He was given his father's second house as a wedding present, so their first major hurdle was overcome with veritable ease. Throughout their forty years of marriage, Archibald had remained impervious to the peevish and selfish wishes of what turned out to be most demanding wife. As far as he was concerned, it was most certainly a case of snappy ever after. Her totally devoted husband managed to keep his equilibrium simply by satisfying her every whim. This done, he was then free to spend a few evenings a week among congenial folk up at "Fennessy's Pub" Sundays he reserved for a pleasant sojourn at South's Pub among the amiable company of friends, following Mass at St. Joseph's Church. After his death Henrietta transferred her demanding nature over to a completely protective nature in regards to her beloved son, Lionel. She was determined, and so unlike her as it turned out, that no girl was going to grab her son simply for his money. She had become so possessive over the past few years, one might say she was jealous of the very bones of her son. "Lionel" she called again in her accustomed high-pitched tone."Come up, I want to talk to you." "Yes Mother," he replied in a less than resigned tone. When he finished his brandy he deftly rinsed out his glass, dried it and replaced it on the drinks cabinet again so that there would be no tell tale signs the following morning. He then popped a Foxes Glacier Mint into his mouth and urgently rotated it therein. He was ever conscious of his mother's insinuations and stinging accusations.

Ascending the deep pile carpeted stairs he gave his usual gentlemanly tap before entering his mother's bedroom. Henrietta was sitting up mid a bevy of fluffy pillows reading from one of Dickens' famous novels, "Little Dorrit". Her silvery-white hair, which during the day she wore neatly piled up in a bun, hung loosely about her shoulders. Removing her glasses she held them aside in one hand while at the same time beckoning to her son to come thither. "Lionel," she began "I want to have a serious chat with you, but first I want you to fetch me a mug of hot cocoa and remember only two and a half spoons of sugar, no more no less". "Yes Mother," sighed Lionel. Then just as he was about to close the bedroom door behind him she called "Hot, Lionel remember not lukewarm." While the kettle was on the boil, Lionel fidgeted about the scullery doing nothing in particular. Then lighting up a cigar he mused to himself, Now what can be so important at this late hour that mother stayed awake to talk to me, maybe its about her will. "Hot, very hot, not lukewarm" he muttered to himself as the boiling water sputtered madly from out the spout. It was in a far more ponderous mood that he ascended the steep stairs for the second time that night. Upon entering his mother's bedroom he walked over and handed her the mug of hot cocoa. Then, just as he was about to sneak away he was arrested mid–step by his mother's instruction to "Sit". "Now Lionel," she began, "I'm not getting any younger." Lionel nodded, thinking happily to himself it must be about the will "I'd like to see you settled down" she continued looking at him rather quizzically. Lionel shifted his position uneasily. "Now I know you have been seen with the odd girl, so I'd like you to make sure you choose the right one. I mean you don't want to end up with a high flyer, who only wants you for your money and the security that follows, do you now son?" "No Mother" sighed Lionel feeling like a bird trapped in a cage. "You know," she continued while sipping gently from her mug of cocoa, "I have an age old test that will reveal whether or not a girl is extravagant. Believe me son it never fails." "And what's that?" queried Lionel " Oh, tut tut I cant tell you that" she replied "That's top secret." "Anyway' she went on "Who are you serious about?" "Well" dawdled Lionel; "There's a few really. I alternate between two every second night and I meet another on weekends." Then, anticipating his mothers questioning glare he continued "Oh don't worry Mother, I go to different places and none of them have so far found out yet." "That's my Lionel, clever boy" she said "So unlike your poor father, he hadn't one iota of social acumen, saved it all for work I imagine." 'Anyway', she went on "Aren't you going to tell me who they are?" "Well" replied Lionel " There's Claire, Brenda, and the best looking of them is Dawn." "You know," said Henrietta "If you intend to marry, you'd want to move soon. It's not good for a man to be alone and if you keep rotating between those three you'll eventually earn a name for yourself and not a very good one I can tell you."

Lionel did not relish that final dig, a bit rough he thought "Now Lionel," she continued in a more condescending tone, while scraping the remaining sugar from the bottom of the mug. "If you were to arrange to have them meet me here over the next few weeks I'll soon tell you whose' who. Just a simple test, they'd have to help in the preparation of the dinner." At that point Lionel winced. 'Don't worry son " she admonished. "Don't you know the best way to get to know anyone properly is in an ordinary situation, not stiff and starchy sitting at table where everyone is at their best. Let each one come of a Sunday, then you can go up to "Fennessey's" for an hour or two as not to be awkwardly hanging around." "Well to tell the truth mother" he confided "I've been a little worried of late wondering about the same matter. You know girls these days, all they seem to want is a good time at some poor man's expense." "Actually son" Henrietta concluded, "There's a second slight test which I'll conduct by observing each one partake of a meal. Believe me Lionel there's method in my madness." With these final words of comfort Lionel took his leave and went to bed.

It was over a month later when Lionel eventually got the courage to broach the matter of dinner with mother to Claire. She jumped at the prospect with the enthusiasm of a greyhound about to bolt from his trap on the evening of the Derby at Harold's Cross. At first this reaction made Lionel happy and then it made him wonder. Could it be that Claire was one step ahead of him? The following Sunday. dawned cool, crisp and dry. Claire awoke with delight in anticipation of meeting Lionel's mother. Lionel picked her up at eleven thirty as they pulled up outside "Lilac Tree." Claire remarked "My, but don't you have a huge house, Lionel, must cost a fortune to keep it up." Just as he was about to fall into the trap of telling her that such things mattered little to him, he suddenly stopped short. His mother's powerful influence over him was beginning to surface. Henrietta answered and greeted them both amicably. Claire's initial impression was that Mrs. Webster was rather formal, yet polite for all that. 'Come inside my dear,' she said 'Lionel's been telling me all about you. We'll have to get to know each other better, wont we?' 'Yes, yes indeed' replied Claire timidly. "Now Lionel" she said turning to her son, "You go along. I told your Uncle Herbert you'd meet him for a round of golf. Dinner will be served at three o clock. Don't be late." With that Lionel took his leave, trusting Claire into the safe and secure clutches of his mother. "Now dear follow me" said the silver haired elderly lady. Claire followed in docile manner, all the while completely bewildered at the sheer enormity and grandeur of the house. Taking three steps down to the scullery Henrietta told the very much taken aback girl to grab a knife and help her with the peeling of the potatoes. "Tis the arthritis beginning to set in" she added. Instrinctively, Claire knew better not to refuse. While in the act of peeling the potatoes, which were soon destined to surround the joint of roast beef already in the oven, Henrietta engaged in ordinary conversation. Claire was completely unaware that she was being closely observed by the sharp eyes of Lionel's mother. Three and half hours later Lionel returned and soon all three were seated to a scrumptious meal of roast beef, gravy, roast potatoes, marrowfat peas, and mashed carrots and parsnips. After the dinner they retired to the parlour for a palatable drink, as Henrietta put it.

The following two Sundays saw the self–same occurrence with Brenda and Dawn. Lionel was beginning to appreciate his mother's obvious astuteness in her manner of observing his three lady friends. According to her-self, Henrietta's plan had worked extremely well and had far exceeded her own expectations. It was the night of the third Sunday, twelve o'clock midnight to be precise, when Henrietta once again heard the front door bang. "Lionel is that you" she called down "Yes mother" he called back "I want to see you," she croaked in an effort to make sure she was heard. "Be right up" called Lionel He ascended the stairs in twos and after the customary tap on the bedroom door, he entered full of anxious anticipation. "Now, not so fast" began the silver haired lady who sat propped up in bed by several soft pillows, "I want you to go down and fetch two double brandies. You and I have something to celebrate. We're about to propose a toast to your future wife" Lionel descended the stairs marvelling at the craftiness of his mother and naturally peppering to find out which one had passed the acid test. He returned promptly and sat on the chair beside her bed. Henrietta, very coolly removed her glasses and slowly placed them in the leather case. She then carefully marked the page where she had finished reading with a bookmark. " Oh but she's tantalising" thought Lionel. "Now Lionel " she began "May I have my drink?" "Sure mother" he replied, handing her the glass. "Here you are, I put a little extra in yours" "How very thoughtful of you," she said, smiling graciously in his direction. .It was then that Lionel noticed his mother's book. She was half way through the "The Fortunes and Misfortunes of Moll Flanders" by Defoe. He had a hazy notion of its contents and wondered at his mother's choice. 'Now' she began I suppose you're anxious to know who it is that passed my test." "Yes, yes of course mother," replied Lionel rather hurriedly.

"It's Dawn the girl I met today." she finally disclosed. "Drop the other two instantly or you'll rue the day, mark my words," Lionel was much relieved and pleased at this disclosure. It was a great consolation to him to know that he was probably going to settle down with a thrifty wife and the fact that Dawn was also quite beautiful he thought would, make him the envy of many a younger man. "But aren't you going to tell me Mother," he queried "How you came to your conclusion."   "No Lionel, I'm not" she replied swirling a measure of brandy around her mouth, while her smiling eyes, akin to one who had trapped its prey, looked far into the distance, "That's my secret."

Henrietta had purposely given each girl some potatoes to peel and had deliberately managed to place a number of bad ones among them; She had spent some time the previous day studying them with her eagle eyes. When Claire came across a slightly bad potato having first cut into it, she simply discarded it whole and entire with no thought of its account. Even when she came upon a potato with only a few 'eyes' she did likewise. Brenda showed only a slight improvement on Claire. She discarded half the potato if it showed any sign of badness. And if she came to one with 'eyes' she would take most of the potato away in her effort to get rid of them giving little or no thought to saving. But Dawn, ah here was the perfect wife for her Lionel. When Dawn encountered a bad part she had cut deftly around it discarding only what was necessary, the same went for the 'eyes'. She cored each one out neatly. And even Henrietta herself was amazed at her sense of thrift. Likewise in the second test while Claire and Brenda had merely pecked at the scrumptious dinner pretending to be ladylike and polite, Dawn had entered heartily into full participation of the meal. There wasn't a morsel left on her plate. "Ah", thought Henrietta earlier that day, "that's the girl for my Lionel". Because as surely as she likes to enjoy her food she will likewise cook a good and substantial meal. My Lionel will have no fears there after a hard day's work. As for the other two they'd be too busy doing themselves up and parading the town, for she had also observed that both of them had brightly painted, longer than long nails. Ah yes, she mused, when Lionel had gone to bed it will be to my own advantage too, for when Dawn marries my Lionel she will be moving into 'Lilac Tree'. Then I can relax in the thought of having three good meals a day for the rest of my life. She had, in a word, outfoxed her son without his ever being the wiser of her devious goings on.

Measley's Metamorphosis

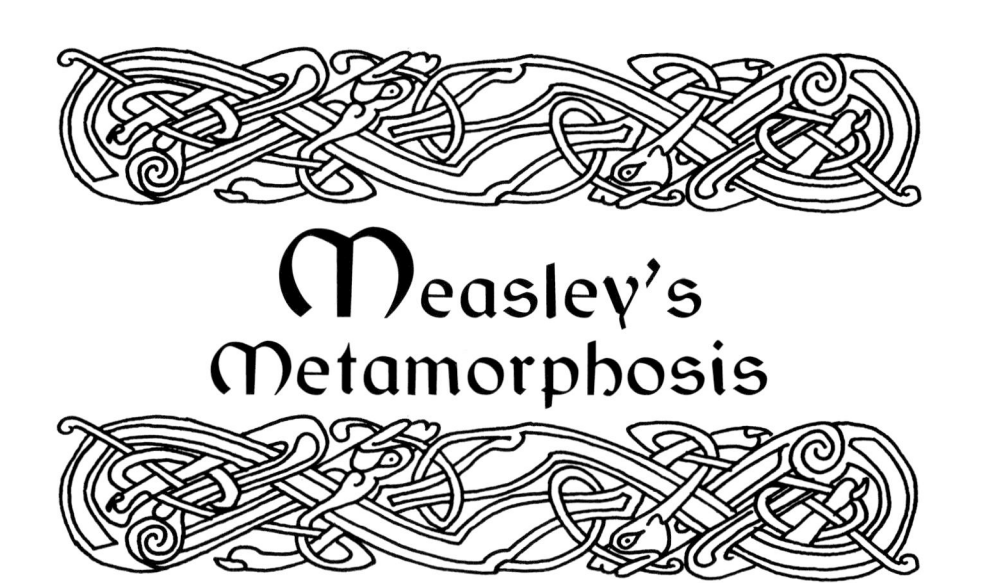

"Measly" McGrath moved stealthily outside his pub counter to shut his front door firmly after the last of his three regular customers had gone. In his wake, he gave a worthless spit, a dismissive gesture, which was also meant for the two men who had departed his premises a few minutes earlier. "Measly" was not his real name but one he had earned and duly bestowed upon him by those whose misfortune it was to have any dealings with the man. He was a misfortunate, miserable creature, a mean specimen of humanity, who had one outstanding aim in life, don't give! No matter what or to whom, just don't give! If, by some mistake, he were to light one of his own matches and share the light with someone else, he would spend the rest of the year regretting it. As we shall see, the name "Measly" was well earned. The pub he owned was called "Crispin's Kiln" and it stood bleakly on the outskirts of the village of Kilkishen in County Clare. The only reason he opened the pub was because it was left to him buy his Godfather, Crispin. It was laid down in the will that the new owner, Crispin McGrath, would keep the pub open, but only between the hours of ten and eleven or eleven-thirty, depending on the season. His granduncle, Crispin, was called that name because his father was a shoemaker and the saint of that name was the patron saint of that exalted art. As a young man, the present owner of the pub was a particular favourite of his grand-uncle, for upon close scrutiny, young Crispin was found to possess qualities which greatly appealed, above all sobriety. The present owner of "Crispin's Kiln" was then a man of some sixty-five years of age. However at first glances one would have given him ten more years. He was very bent from the unmannerly, one might even say backward practise of never looking anyone directly in the eye and being low of stature didn't help in his case at all. He spoke in a near whisper, just one of his saving qualities, reluctant to even give the pleasure of his voice to any one. He wore the self-same pair of hob-nailed boots for the past twenty-five years and when they called for soles or heels he successfully accomplished the task all by himself. And in an effort to "make" out of this three regulars he would drain every drop from the left-over glasses and by the end of the week manage at least one half pint for himself. Cigarettes, not fully smoked, would, in his own good time, be collected, emptied out, gathered and re-rolled to afford himself a smoke or two once a week. For "Measly", this was victory over his fellow man. Now it was commonly known that "Measly" McGrath was a wealthy man and the conversation often ran "Who in God's name was he saving his wealth for?' He had no family. Rumour had it that forty years previously he was wed to a Masie McIntyre. It was a marriage arranged by a matchmaker, but alas, when poor Crispin found out on his wedding night that he had to give something of himself he restrained himself. And the very next day, so the story ran, Masie McIntre was sent packing, bag and baggage back to Drombanna, from whence she had come only a day or two previously.

"Measly" McGrath ran his pub like no other in or around Kilkishen. He opened on the dot of ten o'clock every night, not one second before and none second after. He denied himself the luxury of electricity and made full use of the common wax candle to light his way in the dark. In the pub, his fire every night consisted of three sods of turf and no more than that, despite the fact that he was known to have plenty of good black turf piled high behind his cottage. It was just as well that "Measly" lived alone because being of an extremely obstinate nature, no one either man or woman could have suffered him. He appeared to have a positive aversion to women and not one dared set foot inside his premises. They would do so at their peril, for it was clearly envisaged what the ice-cold reception might be. For poor "Measly" McGrath was most definitely a human misfortune, of whose nature it was to create chasms between himself and his fellow human beings instead of building bridges to reach them. He had a pitiful, suspicious nature and suspected the motives of anyone who tried to get on friendly speaking terms with him. Perish the thought of exchanging gifts at the festive season or any other time of the year. That was anathema to "Measly" McGrath.

How was it then, one may ask, that three villagers made his pub their local. Perhaps the name "Crispin's Kiln" attracted at least two of them but what of the third? The first of these brave characters was Michaeline Ryan, nicknamed the "Smithy" for he was indeed the very popular village blacksmith and part of his job of course was, working with fire. The second Simon O'Grady, nicknamed "Stoker" because of his job on the old steam train, which ran from Limerick to Dublin and back again. But the third, Pajoe Lynch who was nicknamed the "Drover" because of his job of driving cattle to the mart, now the reason for his nightly visits to "Crispins Kiln" was a real puzzle indeed. Each of them, in any case would arrive individually on the seven nights of the week. They knew enough just to say, "Good night Crispin' to which each would receive a begrudging nod of the head which on occasions was coupled with a distant somewhat icy emission of eye contact. Conversation on most night was conducted between Stoker Drover and Smithy. Occasionally, "Measly' would emit a grunt from inside the counter. The three regulars never quite knew if this gesture meant approval or disapproval and to be honest about it, they cared less. They enjoyed their pints of Guinness in quiet surroundings and that was basically why they came there every night. One thing was certain, "Measly" McGrath had no need to go into the village to find out what was going on, for, being skilled in the art of listening, he knew the comings an goings of everyone by putting his well-tainted ears to work. As well as being left the pub, cottage and land, "Measly" McGrath was also left by his granduncle for his pleasure, a fine old record player, the kind you had to wind up. Around the time this story took place he was the proud possessor of three John McCormack records, "Kathleen Mavourneen", "The Rosary" and "Genevieve". On Friday, Saturday and Sunday nights, Measly insisted on playing the three records in rotation, then back over again and again. Stoker, Smithy and Drover often wished that the needle would break, for besides suffering the woeful monotony of the three songs, the crackly frying eggs and rashers quality, grated slightly on their nerves. It goes without saying that during these musical sessions their conversation was much curtailed, if not, they were in danger of being the recipients of a grunt and an icy stare. And so, as they sat and consumed their pints of Guinness, many an understanding glance would be exchanged among the three of them.

As stated at the outset, "Measly" McGrath had just bolted his pub door for the night, having emitted this customary spit on the stone floor in an act of worthless dismissiveness to his three regular customers .It was a complete source of wonder as not a small amount of annoyance, how these three men could waste their hard earned money on such good a useless commodity as liquor, useless liquor that he deducted, served little purpose but to soften the brain and lessen the pocket. The night in question was in nineteen hundred and fifty-four. The sky expelled a greyness, which was in keeping with the season. The previous day had been dull and bitingly cold .It was hardly surprising then that a swarm of swirling snowflakes greeted the pub owner as he opened his back door to make his weary way over to his cottage. As he did so, and despite the inclemency of the elements, he wasted no time but used that short walk to cogitate with himself on how he has spent the day. He carefully assessed that he hadn't transgressed his maxims even in the minutest detail and that included not even giving a hint of a smile to anyone, for it is a well established fact, that when we decide to smile at someone, we give part of ourselves away.

Once inside his cottage door, Measly got a nasty fright, for through the dimness, he noticed the swift movement of a small creature. Upon further inspection, he was horrified to realise that the mouse which had just scurried from the table in an effort to find an exit, had been politely feeding on his goodly lump of Gorgonzola cheese. Measly had to think quickly. No mouse was going to get the better of him while he slept, so he reluctantly decided to finish off the remainder of the cheese. Now whether it was the consumption of such an amount of cheese before retiring or the night that was in it, November Eve, but a strange occurrence ensued the very minute Measly's head hit the pillow.

He suddenly found himself the special guest of a troupe of the wee folk who occupied a well-known fairy fort on a by road which ran adjacent to the village. Head of the merry troupe was the snow white, long- bearded, Mezmerick. At the snap of his tiny fingers, everyone moved, meticulously carrying out his every order. Some others were named, Wenslot, Lowlet, Weeanda, Tubbylana, Hoppyanna and Fairyana. After being ushered into their awesome verdant enclosure, Measly was immediately seated on a plush bright red chair which he barely fitted into. A drink of crimson hue contained in an excellently cut-glass tumbler was placed in his hand, becoming almost lost in the process of being enclosed in his ample fist. As he sipped from the drink, the palatable taste of which he had never before experienced, the wee folk sang and danced for his pleasure to the dulcet music of several harps. Measly was simply ecstatic. At Mezmeric's bidding, Tubbylana replenished the guest's tumbler with the crimson-coloured drink. Measly smiled for one of the very few times in his life, he even rejoiced with the wee dancers and singers. He had to pinch himself hard a few times to ensure this was all really happening.

The suddenly and with out warming, the music ceased and so did the joyful intonations;
> "We are the merry wee folk
> Happy as can be folk
> Love to hop and skip around
> God help big folk who touch our ground!"

Mezmerick was seen to ever so cagily peer out through a slight gap in one if the many thick bushes which surrounded their secluded enclosure. Instantly, he drew back, wiping monstrous beads of sweat from his wee forehead with what appeared to be a large green handkerchief but which was a actually a recently plucked dog-leaf. "Oh, god of all Fairies" he shrieked "What can this mean?" Outside their happy enclosure he had seen, what appeared like, a village of very angry people, lead by Measly's three regular customers, Smithy, Stoker and Drover. Everyone carried dangerous looking instruments. Some had shovels, some had hoes, some had slashooks, while others bore pitchforks and scythes. They were a band of very angry people. Mezmerick slowly ventured his head out through the self-same gap once again, hesitantly enquiring from the leaders of the angry group what their grievance might be. "Oh" blurted out Smithy "That mean, measly character you hold in your clutches, everyone hates him." "Yes" continued Stoker, in equally angry voice "He's too mean to light a warm fire' 'And,' broke in Drover waving his sharp scythe "He's too mean even to smile" The three leaders were bad enough, but when Mezmerick witnessed the near madness of the other villagers, he all but fainted on the spot. "Let us at him" they shouted in unison" We'll scalp him, the mangey 'oul scrounger."

While all this was transpiring outside the enclosure, Measly experienced a tinge of fright which quickly heightened causing him to shake all over. Then suddenly, they gained entrance all as one and began physically attacking the wee folk's guest. He was totally engulfed beneath their fierce anger and dangerous weapons. "God in heaven, God in Heaven, what's happening?" yelled a much-perspired Measly, as he clung to the one corner of his bed-sheet, which hadn't yet been mangled. He lay there mesmerised, thinking of the overnight happenings and vowing never again to eat Gorgonzola cheese before going to bed. This was certainly one case where his extreme meanness served him an evil blow.

"Damn that mouse," he muttered "'Twas all his fault, so it was". As Measly lay helplessly stretched out on the bed, he thought deeply about the events of the past few hours "I wonder" he thought seriously, "Do people hate me that much, can people be the object of hate without even realising it?" As he mulled and mulled over that possibility, he gradually came to the conclusion, "Yes" he thought "I'm only living for myself and who will get all my riches when I die?. The pub doors will be shut forever, It will eventually rot away to nothing. Were the wee folk in their own way passing on a message of good will to me? Unbeknown to me, they might be my friends, after all," he thought.

Bleary-eyed and still quite numb, he held his head with both hands. His mind constantly reverted back to the previous night's strange occurrences. It was all so real he recalled. Poor "Measly" shook his head again and again. Then suddenly, like a bolt of fork lightning, he jumped out of bed, lifted up the mattress, and grabbed a few bundles of fifty-pound notes. After his breakfast, he got the bus into Limerick. There he purchased a new suit, shirt, jumper and shoes. He also bought an ample supply of groceries. He contacted the E.S.B. about installing electricity. He assured them he didn't care what it cost. When he returned home he immediately went into the pub and lit a huge big turf fire. He then brought in two large tea chests full of turf to keep the fire replenished at all times. He walked into the village and called upon an old school friend, Charlie Hayes. Although very surprised, Charlie greeted him amicably.
"Measly" invited him up to his pub that night. Happy in himself, he thought on the way back, ah well, it's a start isn't it. Back at the pub, he set about dusting and tidying. He polished his black, hob-nailed boots and looked forward to opening earlier than usual. He did in fact open at eight o'clock and he had a blazing fire alight when his three regular customers arrived at their usual time. He even managed to say "hello" to each one of them in turn. Gradually, poor "Measly" was walking up to life and to all the natural graces that this life is heir to. Stoker, Smithy and Drover assumed their usual places and ordered their pint. As "Measly"

went over to replenish the fire with turf, the three regulars couldn't believe their eyes but judged it better not to voice their disbelief. Before the night was out, Measly invited his three loyal customers to come and join him in a double brandy each. Having never before heard their barman speak above a mere whisper, they marvelled at the fine manly, resonant, voice he possessed.

As the night wore on, every empty glass was replenished again and again. Measly reached up to a top shelf inside the counter and rescued a vintage whisky of long years standing and when his customers left, partook of an ample share of it. And as he reminisced on his frugal days the brightly burning fire roared madly up the chimney. With little thought the safety. Measly shuffled his way over to his cottage about three in the morning. As soon as his head hit the pillow, he knew no more until he was rudely awakened by two hours later by an urgent banging on his cottage door, 'Get up, get up Measly" roared the local guard 'There's a big fire at the pub' Measly being quite unaccustomed to strong drink took a long time to register as would have normally been expected of him. He was holding his head with both his hands as the guard continued to shout 'fire fire' when he finally arrived over to see his pub in a cauldron of roaring flames he was visibly devastated. .He, the very essence of sobriety was now bearing witness to a spectacle caused by nothing else but sheer carelessness which was occasioned by intoxicating drink. The damage caused by the fire proved irreparable today a shell replaced his beloved pub, yesterday's lifeline.

Measly McGrath lived out the remainder of his days a broken man. He came to realise a dear, dear lesson, which we all might learn from. If you are happy in your own little niche doing what you want to do the way you want to do it, don't change, But particularly don't change for the sake of other people. You might rue the day as poor Measly did.

Twice, she came a-cropper

A single lady of high moral standing lived near the cosy and thriving town of Ennis. Her name was Kate O'Grady and she was known for miles around as simply Miss O'Grady. Now Miss Kate O'Grady lived on a stretch of road between Spancilhill and Ennis, called the Tulla Road. Her snow-white thatched cottage was remarked on by several passers-by, for what with the annual whitewash and the striking emerald green windowsills and doors, it really was most eye-catching. Miss Kate O'Grady was well schooled in many good homemaking crafts, such as jam-making, and cheese making. She always kept four goats, three of which she milked twice daily. Her bread and cake making was of the finest ever tasted. In fact every year on the twenty-third of June, no matter what the weather, she managed to get to the traditional Horse fair at the Cross-of Spancilhill. She would bring along with her three large boxes. One contained currant cakes, a second contained several rounds of soda bread, while a third contained an amount of cheese which she had made from the pure and nutritious goats milk. If one farmer didn't give her a lift there, then another would. Kate O'Grady was a most welcome sight at Spancilhill every year. The hungry men made light work of her goodies and Kate would arrive home all the richer. But before boarding the neighbouring farmer's car she would make her way a quarter of a mile down the road to "Duggan's " famous pub. Here, at her own request the usually straight-laced lady would drink a pint of stout as she listened to the earthy occupants'rousing choruses, led by bodhran and flute. This was her one and only drink until June the twenty-third the following year. Onlookers side glanced as the respected lady, who sat tall and erect savouring every drop of the black stuff.

It was Kate O'Grady's practise to go into Ennis town on the day after the fair, to bank her previous day's takings. The only time this did not occur was if the day after the fair was a Saturday or a Sunday. In that case she would sleep with the box of money under her pillow. Then at the earliest possible chance on the Monday morning she was to be seen walking to Ennis town and the Lord God almighty couldn't be persuaded to give the maiden lady a lift.

Once inside the bank she would request to speak to the manager, who was well acquainted with Kate O'Grady's ways. The reason for this request was that he, Mr. Grump and no one else would transact her financial affairs. As she would confide in him, I don't want my monetary gain of yesterday to be the topic of conversation in this town. Mr Grump would merely smile understandingly in reply, not even going so far as to try to explain to the lady their very high standard of confidentiality. Business having been successfully and most discreetly transacted, Mr Grump would rise to hold the door open for Kate O'Grady as she made her swift getaway, usually with her head slightly bent. No visit to Ennis town would be complete without a visit to her favourite eating house on O'Connell Street. 'Brogan's.' Here the good lady enjoyed a pot of tea and two currant scones, which she lavished with good country butter. Today, the day being in it, she decided to have their delicious four course meal. She relished the sumptious food with all her might and having paid her bill left the restaurant much gruntled.

Now Kate O'Grady not only sat tall, but walked even taller, no dowager's hump for her. So on this fateful day as she rounded a certain corner, she tripped on a slightly jutting flagstone outside a building which had recently been renovated. Well, down she came a cropper, hat and all. Two men who were passing by, quickly aided her to her feet and then she continued just a little more cautiously on her journey home.

Once landed, she removed her hat and coat for although it was the month of June, the weather was inclement enough even for a fire. Kate made a mug of strong tea and sat down, put her feet up and pondered and pondered. Something was niggling at her brain, which was at this particular time, overheating. What could it be? Ah yes she recalled to herself Didn't I see in 'The Clare Champion' a few months ago where a farmer who dropped down an uncovered manhole and injured himself took action, won the case and received for himself a substantial sum of money. And so, as she slowly sipped on her mug of well-brewed tea, something was brewing in Kate O'Grady's mind.

What if I took action? What if I won? Now with a substantial sum of money she assured herself, I would have to go to Limerick to bank it. Even Mr. Grump wouldn't be made the wiser of that financial windfall.

Now as she pondered, she finally decided to feign an injured elbow. She would have all the points written down, how she had untold trouble milking the goats, how she was unable to stir with her usual vehemence when making her cheese, how her bread was never the same due to kneading almost entirely with her left hand. All this was costing her dearly, and it was all the fault of these very careless builders, whose haphazard work was the cause of her falling.

So two days later found Kate O'Grady in Ennis on very important private business. She had studied the list of four solicitors practising in the town at the time. She decided to choose the youngest, Mr. Theodore Fletcher. .He might be anxious to gain a name for himself and therefore might not probe too deeply into her mishap. She rang the doorbell with the finger of her left hand, for due to prior meditation she had placed her right hand in a home-made sling. From now on, she must act the part. 'Oh good day!' she greeted the receptionist, 'May I see Mr.Fletcher?' 'Yes of course dear', answered the receptionist. 'May I please have your name?' 'Miss Kate O'Grady' ' she answered 'And not Mrs' 'Thank you kindly' answered the receptionist. 'You are indeed most helpful'.

Kate O'Grady found herself for the first time in a solicitors office. 'Now what can I do for you' enquired Mr. Fletcher. The injured lady duly briefed the good man on how incapacitated she had become since her terrible mishap. 'Oh dear!' sighed the solicitor. 'That is financially crippling indeed'. Having entered all the necessary details in his book,he informed Miss O'Grady that he would be filing a complaint to the errant builders and that she would be hearing from him within a fortnight. Mr Fletcher gave her hope of a settlement in fairly substantial terms. It would not be necessary to visit a doctor or a hospital he told her as neither could appreciate her private incapacity.

Kate O'Grady continued her work at home, but at a lesser capacity so that anyone could say, yes, things had slowed somewhat. True to his word, at the end of two weeks she received a typed letter from the solicitor informing her that proceedings had now begin against the faulty builders and that she would be appearing at Ennis district court on the last day of July.

Kate O'Grady anticipated the event with positive enthusiasm. Although she now had decide that three fourths of the award would go immediately into the bank in Limerick, she would use the rest to purchase a half acre more and invest in a few more goats and a cow or two. She had continuously rationalised her injury in her own mind. She even managed to make things look worse by replacing the strong cotton sling with a leather one. This, she thought would look the real thing in court.

Well, finally the long awaited day arrived. It was a dull rainy day. She got a lift into town. Her case was scheduled for 11.15 a.m. In no way did she feel nervous. She felt extremely confident. As she entered the court room she noticed two men in overalls, sitting down. They were guarding a stone slab, which she recognised, was exactly like the one she had fallen over. A template of the offending stone slab was required to be brought to the courts on the day of the case. So it was that the two men arrived outside the court very early with their wheelbarrows. Far they were from blessing the 'injured' lady. We can only imagine their concern as they waited in the rain for the court to open.

At precisely 11.15 a.m. on the last day of July on the year 1950, the case of Miss Kate O'Grady against the offending builders opened. The preliminaries having been dispersed with. The judge Mr Harvey Dore, queried 'Now tell me my dear lady on the day in question were you in any way inebriated? Well, it's a good thing that looks don't kill or this good judge would never judge again. "No, I certainly wasn't" Miss O'Grady answered emphatically. This reply occasioned a look of approval from Mr Theodore Fletcher. "And you say" continued Judge Dore 'That this injured elbow has greatly affected your home business'. The lady in the 'box' entertained the court for the next twenty minutes, as she minutely itemised the many handicaps she experienced as a result of her fall. She also informed the court of a drastic financial drop. Mr Theodore Fletcher interjected many a supporting remark. He and she were of the one mind, well almost. The only dividing line being an enthusiastic solicitor that was duped into believing his client had suffered extreme injury, whereas she had not.

The judge sounded somewhat sympathetic, if at times he looked a little puzzled, "And" continued Judge Dore, "You live alone?" Miss Kate O'Grady answered in the affirmative. According to her and the solicitor, things were getting hot, only a matter of moments really. Judge Dore remained silent for the space of one full minute, during which time he kept his head bent as if in deep thought. The silence in the courtroom was awesome and admirable. On resuming, the judge said rather hastily, 'I wonder Miss O'Grady would you kindly remove your hat before I relate my decision?' Kate was so excited that quick as a flash and without thinking she put up her right hand took off the pin and removed her hat. That did it!

 This action was accomplished with the greatest of ease, much to Judge Dore's delight and the surprise of all present. 'My dear woman,' he continued 'Go, in God's holy name and stop trying to defraud good hardworking people' He then continued, 'Go home and milk your goats, make your cheese and knead all the dough you want.' Kate O'Grady stepped down and left the courtroom, rather ashamed. Hardly stopping to look at Theodore Fletcher, her loyal solicitor, she had indeed come a cropper for the second time in the space of two months.

Jimin

"Isn't it about time Jimin that you started lookin' for a wife" said Nora Stritch in her usual taunting manner. She eyed him across the wooden table with her close-set, steely blue eyes. Jimin continued to crack open his second duck egg. Then without even pretending he had heard his mother's well-meant remark, he took a large bite of brown home made bread, which he immediately followed by an impatient gulp from his cream, blue–striped mug of strong tea. "Did ya hear me, Jimin?" she reiterated sharply. Without even looking in her direction, Jimin gave a bare nod of acknowledgement. "Ya know I'm not getting any younger and I'd like for to leave this world knowin' that you're content and well taken care of," she continued. Jimin, who was now almost forty-five had received this selfsame maternal prod almost every day since he turned forty. Unbeknown to his mother, he was studying that situation very carefully, but an innate wisdom told him that the time was not yet ripe. He considered himself far too young for that sort of caper.

Jimin and his mother Nora lived in a fine old cottage in an isolated spot outside Cree, a village a few miles from the thriving town of Kilrush. Being an only child, for Nora was forty when she had married, Jimin had been a real pet ever since he saw the light of day and was still considered such upon approaching middle age. His father had died two years previously. .He had always been less protective of his son and often wished they had more in family. Steven Stritch had always been a hard working man on the farm. Unfortunately he was of a stubborn nature to the extreme that he weathered even the most inclement elements. Finally he succumbed to the flu which progressed to pneumonia, which eventually took him. Since Steven's death Jimin had been a source of great consolation to his mother working the farm every day from dawn till dusk. She got her freshly–laid duck eggs and hen eggs and plenty of milk from Lucy the nanny Goat. Her days were mainly occupied with sweeping the kitchen floor several times. Often she would sweep it six times in the space of one half hour. One might say she was of a nervous disposition. In between sweeping, she would sit by the turf fire on the old wicker chair and puff constantly on her old clay pipe. At times such as these she would keep her mug replenished with strong tea that she poured from the earthenware tea pot, which was constantly kept hot on the hob.

Lately, her agitation seemed to reach a crescendo. She feared for Jimin as he now approached his forty-fifth birthday. As she puffed nervously on her clay pipe she cogitated with herself. Wasn't there Josie, Joe Slattery, the blacksmith's daughter, a fine broth of a woman, she never ever went with a fella,. She could make him a fine hot stew, bake him soda bread and his favourite spotted dick. Then wasn't there the tailor Robbie Stark's daughter Jenny, she must be easily twelve stone, another fine broth of a girl .She could wash and sew for him .She could carry in heavy buckets of coal and turf from the back as good as any man. And he'd be assured of a fine suit of clothes for the wedding for half nothing'. And what of Molly, John Dillon, the undertaker's daughter. Now there was a girl for her Jimin. Oh what heavenly light shone from out those two bright blue eyes. Sure she was reputed to have two knocked knees but that should not prove an obstacle to the cleaning and the cooking and the washing and the ironing. 'O God!' she sighed as she knocked out the leftover ash from the hob and took up the sweeping brush for about the twentieth time that morning, 'I'll have to have a serious chat with St Jude'.

'Is that you son?' she called after hearing the back door bang. 'Yes Mother' came the manly reply. 'A bloody awful day for working on the farm Ma', he greeted her as he entered the small cottage kitchen to the welcome aroma of bacon and cabbage. 'Whisht now Jimin' she cautioned as she bent over to remove the hot plates from the hob. 'Don't be usin' them bad words, your poor father God rest him wouldn't like it now Jimin would he?" Shaking out his cap Jimin timorously replied, 'I suppose not Ma' then under his breath he muttered 'I didn't know dead people could hear'. During dinner Jimin got the usual gruelling admonition about finding himself a wife. 'I'm not getting any younger son,' she reminded him. He spooned almost a quarter of country butter from the plate and flopped it on top of his piping hot spuds, which he had just relieved of their jackets. 'Yes Ma' replied Jimin trying to remain patient 'None of us are.' 'Watch it now Son,' she retorted 'Don't be getting cheeky, I'm your mother you know'. Jimin swallowed down a huge gulp of milk to wash down his dinner 'What about Josie Slattery ?' Nora taunted her love sluggish son. 'She'd make you grand wholesome stews, now wouldn't that be just grand Jimin, wouldn't it?' 'She's fifty' muttered

Jimin 'Fifty now, fifty is that so?' Remarked Nora 'Then you have slight interest there now have you Jimin?' 'No,' replied Jimin flatly. Removing his cap from the hob, he quickly made his exit.

Jimin Stritch was a fine sturdy block of a man who possessed a thick crop of kinky greying hair. With huge strong forearms his one passion in life was the farm work and making that work pay so as to keep thc home fires burning. He loved his home and he enjoyed providing for it. Like many of his fellow villagers he owed nothing to no one and that was how he wished it to remain. Jimin was known as the strong, silent type. He didn't exactly light up a roomful of people when he walked in yet, all were genuinely glad to see him when he came into 'The Ould Still' at the weekend. There, in the company of the villagers he enjoyed pint after pint while often playing a game or two of forty five. At other times he would listen carefully to the topic of conversation before adding his commentary. Jimin's opinion was much valued mainly because he didn't often voice it. Jimin Stritch was a very well liked character.

On morning as Jimin sat down to his breakfast he felt he was in for a deluge of questions, How right he was and how well he could read his mothers mood from her fidgety movements. 'Now Jimin,' she began, 'Have you thought of a suitable wife yet?' 'No Mother' was the flat weary-filled reply. 'And what about Mollie Dillon?' she needled 'Wouldn't we all be sure of a fine burial now wouldn't we', 'Who cares when you're dead' mumbled Jimin through a mouthful of porridge. 'What's that ya said?' questioned Nora tartly 'I said I wouldn't care to be dead," replied Jimin 'Any way, Mollie has lovely blue eyes and they say she is great at the cleaning' she reminded her disinterested son. 'She's fifty three Ma,' he said very definitely looking directly at his mother as he wiped his mouth with a large blue and white handkerchief. With that he was gone out the back door to the farm. During the course of the morning Nora became her usual agitated self alternating between sweeping and clay pip smoking. "I'm getting more and more worried about that young fellow of mine," she said to herself "I wonder if he has any eye for a woman at all."

The following morning saw a repetition of the previous morning. Lucky for Nora her son was a patient man. Another might have left fly at her long ago. 'Well Jimin and how's your cold today?" she queried 'Fine mother, just fine, the ould drop of brandy is a great cure-all,' he replied rather chirpilly 'And what about the half bottle of Sloan's Liniment left over after your poor father,' she said 'I put it on the floor near your bed last night'. 'Oh that must have been what I knocked over as I stumbled into bed then' he said. Nora decided to change the subject. 'Did you ever hear tell of a Jenny Stark, you know the tailor's daughter?' 'Yes' mumbled Jimin 'She's flat chested and fifty." 'What's that?' queried Nora, 'I said she's fat and thrifty,' he replied. 'Now wouldn't she make a grand wife for you Jimin?' persisted Nora. Jimin continued to dig into he second boiled duck egg. 'She's a fine sturdy girl, Jimin' she continued 'She could wash and sew for you. She could darn your socks and sew in your buttons. And I believe she's great at turning in collars and you know how hard you are on shirt collars Jimin' . In his usual listless manner Jimin coolly wiped some of the egg yolk from the side of his mouth and was off like a shot. 'Bye Mother' he called as he secured the latch on the back door behind him.

Now if it was true that Jimin Stritch was slow with words, his thoughts certainly made up for that. The following weekend being the August weekend, Jimin decided to go to Kilkee. He took out his best suit from the camphor smelling wardrobe and he brushed it off. He got out his best blue and white striped shirt and navy tie. He polished his fine pair of Winstanly laced black shoes, hawing on them proudly in the buffing off process, for which he used newspaper. He carefully applied a generous dose of pomade to his fine kinky crop of hair. Having packed his little brown case he bade 'Good Bye' to his mother, telling her to mind herself. Then off with him to the local post office where he withdrew £50 just to be on the safe side. As he boarded the bus at Kilrush he said to himself, "If I don't take this matter in hands that mother of mine will drive me mad." Upon arriving in Kilkee he searched for suitable accommodation. Finally he settled in at 'Bayview' which afforded him an excellent view of the vast expansive ocean. Jimin set out to enjoy himself and that was exactly what he did. There was music every night at the Strand Hotel, so Jimin decided to take full advantage of it while he enjoyed a few drinks. On the final night of his stay as he sat there casually glancing across the room he was suddenly aware of a fine looking girl gazing intently at him. He felt a little awkward, then as she stood to replenish her glass he observed that she had a fine womanly figure, fulsome breasts, rather slim waist, which was neatly belted, and generous, though not fat hips. Sheepishly he gave another glance in her direction and to his amazement she was still looking at him. 'Now there's a fine lass,' he said to himself. "Twenty-five is about all she'd be." And dead right he was too, for as she passed behind his stool on the way out to the ladies she placed her hand on his shoulder and said, 'Are you enjoying yourself there?' Jimin wasn't sure but he thought he felt a slight shiver down his spine. Although somewhat thrilled he became a little nervous and didn't know where to turn. On her return he mustered up just enough courage to extend her a good wholesome wink. That did it. Quick as a flash she relocated herself and her glass right over beside him. They got talking and Jimin found himself very much at ease with the long blonde haired girl from Limerick. As the night progressed to the wee hours of the morning, Jimin became firm in his resolution to stay the week. Peggy O'Dea was staying in the Esplanade on the Strand line. The following day Jimin sent a card to his mother informing her of his prolonged stay. That week was like paradise for Jimin. Peggy told him she was a teacher in Limerick but that in September she was securing a place in a school in Kilrush run by the nuns. Jimin and Peggy became fast friends. One might say they were well met and satisfied each other's expectations very well.

At the end of the week, Jimin had to return home to Cree. Peggy promised they would meet again when she settled into her digs in Kilrush in a month's time. Jimin went home thrilled and rejuvenated by his unexpected good fortune. 'Well' asked his Mother when he came home that night, 'Did you meet Molly Dillon at all down by the seaside. I heard she was down there for the weekend.' 'No' sighed Jimin wearily 'I didn't meet Molly Dillon or Jenny Stark or Josie Slattery either.' 'Oh,' was all Nora had to say. 'But I did meet a fine looking woman from Limerick, Mother' said Jimin 'You'll get to meet her in a few weeks time." 'And,' queried Nora "Tell me Jimin, can she wash and sew and cook and is she strong enough to bring in the coal and turf?'. 'She's all that Mother and a whole lot more, you'll see'. 'I'm looking forward to meeting her,' said Nora eyeing her son cautiously 'Sure I know son you have the best of good judgement but young men can be very easily led and you must be ever wary. Now mark my words Jimin', she continued 'You're not very well schooled in the ways of the world of women.' 'I am now,' muttered Jimin under his breath.

September dawned and was never before so welcome to Jimin Stritch. As arranged he met Peggy at the Market Square in Kilrush .It was a Saturday afternoon. "Now Peggy" Jimin announced 'I have a big favour to ask of you.' 'Anything, Jimin.' she replied 'I'd like you to meet my mother, Nora.' Jimin begun nervously, "Ive been telling her all about you.", 'Id love to' replied Peggy cheerfully. That evening Nora was sitting by her warm fire smoking her clay pipe and sipping a wee drop of brandy when she was suddenly roused from her sleepy state by the closing of the front door. In came Jimin 'Hello son' she greeted. Then, thinking her eyes were playing tricks on her she said 'Who's that young girl Jimin? Does she want a pinch of tay or sugar?' 'Ma' replied Jimmy cheerfully, "This is Peggy O' Dea, my wife to be within the year'. Nora became flustered, "But,' queried Nora completely taken aback, 'Can she wash and sew and cook?' 'Will you whisht Ma' interrupted Jimin 'What does it avail a full blooded man on a cold winters night after a hard days work whether a wife can wash or sow or cook?' 'Then.' he continued 'A man has other essential needs you know.' Now young Jimin had poor Nora thinking. After taking a slug of her brandy and puffed a few puffs on her clay pipes she looked at him and said, 'You know what Jimin Stritch, I nearly was thinking you couldn't be bothered about that at all. Oh but aren't you the crafty lad that I reared.' Then she gave a wicked sounding cackle of a laugh. She welcomed Peggy warmly and Peggy took to her instantly. From that day forward Jimin never again heard the names of Jenny Stark, Josie Slattery and Molly Dillon within the walls of his home. Without realising it herself, it was Nora who was responsible for the fine young intelligent lass that Jimin now found himself engaged to.

Who killed 'Nettles' Normoyle?

Part 1

The sombre death knell resounded over the secluded and peaceful village of Bruree in the county of Limerick, heralding yet another of its stalwart inhabitants on his journey to the next world. "Nettles" (Ned) Normoyle busied himself by the open grave, making sure that all was in order for the ever-exacting undertaker, Thomas Moroney junior, son of the now much disabled Thomas Moroney whom "Nettles" had faithfully served for the past fifty odd years. Nettles took to the job of gravedigging with gusto and great sense of pride. For him every shovelful of earth carried with it a real sense of meaning, one might say, a delving into the past, a chance to reminisce on life thus far, a chance to ponder on the life of the dear departed one, whose lot it was to be lowered into that particular plot.

Today it was the turn of Anselm Thornhill, a man of considerable personal acumen and not a small amount of wealth. He, together with his wife Isabelle who had predeceased him by two years, lived at the old manor "Marble Halls" just within view of the sweet village where once dwelt a young lad by the name of Eamon de Valera. When joined in holy matrimony Anselm and Isabelle were both bordering on middle age. It was hardly surprising then that no offspring ensued. Having no immediate relatives Anselm Thornhill brought much of his wealth with him to the grave. This was clearly evident from the weight of gold that embellished every finger of both hands as many an avaricious eye viewed the corpse at the wake on the previous night.

In life, Anselm Thornhill had been a most distinguished cut of a man, with well-tapered handlebar moustache, a fine crop of silvery grey hair which never appeared out of place. This was accentuated by unusually lengthy sideburns. A pair of thick, bushy eyebrows protruded above a pair of aristocratic steely blue eyes, which were of an expressive nature. He stood almost six feet tall on his stocking feet and when dressed in his equestrian type outfit, one could easily has mistaken him for an army colonel. He was hardly ever seen without the proverbial blackthorn stick and the turned down pipe, which he seemed to puff on incessantly. He was, however known to release it from between his lips on occasion, particularly if he happened to be engaged in conversation with someone, which entailed pointing to an object in the field beyond. Anselm Thornhill was a most congenial and affable type of gentleman who held firmly to the maxim that all men are created equal, without exception in God's sight. The fact that he was blessed with a super abundance of this world's goods he accepted as a mere accident of birth. It could well have been he thought the village Dinny dimwit who had inherited his naturally acquired wealth. Likewise, he felt that he could have ended up as the village fool if fate had not been kind to him. He knew all too well it was but a hair's breath which separated the twain. In death, Anselm Thornhill retained much of the character he had been blessed with in life. Some were heard to whisper between sips of whiskey, 'Sure doesn't he only look like he is sleeping'.

'Nettles' Normoyle was a man of noticeable seclusion in and around the village of Bruree. He entertained nobody and never allowed himself to be entertained by anybody. He was low of stature but strong of muscle. He had been the only child of Martin and Nannie Normoyle, a couple who had come together on their early forties by means of the local matchmaker, Charlie O'Neill. He was man of self-imposed reclusive persuasion and it didn't take long for would-be intruders to realise that he was most definitely a man apart. It was at your own peril that you courted the favour of his company. The reason for the nickname 'Nettles' is quite simple to explain. For, instead of flowers in his garden leading to his cottage, he cultured an array of wild nettles which he cut down bi-annually to a specific height. But of course, unbeknown to the puzzled masses there was much method in his unexplained madness. He made nettle tea and also used the nasty, prickly weed as part of a recipe for many potions to relieve various troublesome ills which plagued him at times, one being the re-occurrence of arthritis. He was the true and trusted gravedigger and he fully realised he had to be in peak condition, for he, more than most was ever conscious of the fact that 'Lady Death' was no respecter of person and could knock at any door in the village at any hour of the day or night, any day of the month. It was therefore important, that 'Nettles' be well at all times. It would never do to leave an anxious corpse beside his unopened new abode, now would it? Besides the postman there was only one other person who was allowed to Ned's door. That was Molly Muldowney. Molly had the best laying ducks for miles around and her eggs were in constant demand all over. She sold dozens of them weekly in and around her immediate vicinity. The neighbours were very grateful to Miss Muldowney and one of them was 'Nettles'. But although Molly delivered the duck eggs to 'Nettles', she never actually came face to face with him. From her initial visit the arrangement was that 'Nettles' would leave the money under the stone pigeon which stood on top of the outside window sill. Molly would dutifully leave the eggs, which were snugly resting amid a crispy bed of hay in a tin box and collect her money. She would then leave quickly and continue her deliveries on her high Lizzie bike. There were never any hitches.

It was usual for 'Nettles' on the day following a burial to go back to the graveyard and spend a solid half-hour tidying up around the grave, which he had covered in the previous day. He used to refer to this as perfecting the job. Canon Hodgins was the first to notice that Ned had not arrived. It was now five o'clock and darkness was about to cloak the village. Thick flakes of snow swirled about creating a near magical picture in the old churchyard. Canon Hodgins walked about in pensive mood, noting here and there the names of the various headstones. Some had lived a short span of life while others had lived much longer. Some too had wealth in this life while others had barely enough to keep body and soul together. Yet, he reminisced thoughtfully, to this end must we all come, for no one has a lease on life. Perhaps, he thought poor old Ned might have found the trudge through the snow just a little too much. Whatever, he said to himself, sure he'll be here tomorrow for certain. Then suddenly, as if awoken from a dream, he was interrupted by the sound of a loud voice coming from direction of the entrance gate. 'Canon, Canon Hodgins' shouted the village minstrel excitedly and very much out of breath. 'Come quickly come quickly'. 'What is it Cecil, what is it?' queried the anxious priest as he moved hurriedly towards the distraught figure of Cecil. 'Its Nettles' sobbed Cecil uncontrollably, 'he's dead, poor old fella he's dead "tis a case of murder we think.". 'Steady Cecil, steady'cautioned the priest. 'What is it you're after tellin' me?' . Cecil a man of some fifteen stone and a half merely sobbed in reply. Sensing there was something dreadfully wrong, the canon urged Cecil to come inside. Immediately and without uttering a word, he ventured to the cabinet and pored Cecil a glass of brandy. The canon himself did not drink alcohol but he always kept some on hand for special visitors. 'Now slow down and tell me' requested the much-concerned priest. 'Miss Muldowney' blurted out Cecil through fitful tears, 'She went with the duck eggs and found Nettles' door flung open and the snow was swirling inside. There was blood on the snow right outside the door'. At that point the canon sat down to relieve himself of a sudden weakness. He was simply speechless, placing both hands to his forehead in a gesture of extreme desperation. 'She knocked, Canon' continued Cecil, 'And when she got no reply she decided to venture in and there she found poor oul Nettles in a pool of blood with his very own slashook beside his bed. Oh Canon, what are we going to do? 'Tis awful, terrible, so it is' sobbed the sorrowful rotund minstrel. Canon Hodgins remained limp for some time. He then rose from his old leather armchair and with all the authority he could muster told the tearful minstrel to go at once to the Garda station and to relate to them the exact story he had related to him.

Cecil left the priest's house with all the docility of an acolyte serving his first mass. Weeping all the while, he half walked half ran as fast as his poor shocked weary body would take him. When he reached the garda station he knocked feverishly on the rust painted door. 'Come in,' came the gruff voice of the sergeant in command of the village, Athanasius

Nugent. This fine specimen of masculinity bore all the hallmarks of a typical staunch limb of the law representative. With his bushy eyebrows and handlebar moustache and a pair of hands that would do justice to Jack the Giant Killer himself, this man was more often than not, happily avoided than warily approached. He bellowed rather than spoke. And unbeknown to himself, was nick-named 'Noodles', due no doubt to the expert manner in which he conducted his various investigations to date, from tracking down the young lads who stole apples from Maggie Maunsell's orchard to pinpointing an elusive and cunning murderer merely by the fact that he stupidly left behind a certain brand of snuff. One might say by his snuff he was known and eventually tracked down by a detective with most acute nostrils. 'Well what can I do for you?" bellowed Nugent upon sighting the poor snivelling Cecil. 'Oh guard' he blurted out, 'A terrible thing has happened, poor old Nettles is dead and they think that its murder.' By way of reply Sergeant Nugent performed a series of questioning blinks with his large blue cocker spaniel eyes. He then asked, 'How do you know this and who told you to come to me?" "Twas Molly Muldowney that made the discovery sir, she's in bits, used to deliver him the duck eggs every day and I told the Canon and he told me to come to you guard,' he replied and immediately gave an unmerciful sneeze into a large blue and white striped handkerchief. This was instantly followed by a loud boo-hooing 'Oh guard, Tis terrible so it is' Then relenting somewhat from his usual authoritative stance, Nugent gestured to the much aggrieved man to go home and he would follow the matter up. He even gave him a three-penny bit as advance payment in the event that he came up with any clues he might unearth which might prove valuable to the impending investigation. Despite his distressed state of mind, the village minstrel was delighted with this personal touch on behalf of the sergeant. Now Sergeant Nugent was well acquainted with the ways of the village and was fully aware of the silent respect those same villagers held for their hard-working gravedigger. He instinctively knew that this was one nut that must be cracked and speedily too. He needed to muster up every fibre of his intuitive and investigative powers and put them to work. No stone should be left unturned until the mystery of Nettles was solved. And so, to this end he lost no time in contacting his understudy, a man of mild temperament but also a man who possessed shrewd judgement, his name was Justin Blake. Yet, he too came under the amusing scrutiny of some villagers and was nicknamed 'Latchit' because of his almost constant admonition to everyone to be sure to latch their doors at night.

It didn't take long for the two men of the law to descend on the home of the poor misfortunate, murdered man. By the time they arrived at the house the snowy conditions had given way to a very heavy persistent rain. They retrieved the slashook and placed it in a sack. They scrutinised the little shack minutely for any clues, which might ease the laborious task of sorting out who the killer might be. Nettles' humble abode bore all the hallmarks of a frugal existence.

Whoever it was anyway who had killed him, they already had judged him to be a very cunning person indeed. It was made to look as if poor old Nettles had mistakenly stumbled and tumbled on the sharp side of the slashook which cut his throat severely. And if that wasn't a crafty enough act, hadn't an almost empty bottle of poteen been left casually nearby. 'Almost too good to be true' mumbled Detective Sergeant Nugent to himself, 'Does whoever it was that did it think that the law in this village has any scrap of grey matter at all at all?' With that he signalled to his confrere Blake to accompany him back to headquarters. As they wearily trudged back the boreen, Noodles carrying the bag, they were at a loss for words. They had no idea in the wide wide world who to suspect. They were dealing with the gruesome murder of an innocent misfortune who hadn't an enemy that was ever known. Their difficult task was to find out who killed Nettles Normoyle?. It wasn't every day or even every decade that a murder was committed in the village of Bruree. They might as well have Everest to climb, so daunting were the possibilities of finding the culprit.

Being of a strictly religious upbringing, Blake lost no time in invoking the help of the Holy Spirit. That same spirit was the furthest thing from Nugent's mind .He believed in one mode of practise and one alone. That lay in the ruthless seeking out of every male villager's movements the previous night from six o'clock onwards. Upon his shrewd investigation it came about that three of the village men folk were in fact not at their respective homes all that previous night and had not returned until half past five on the following morning. They were Michael O' Flaherty (Eel), Pajoe Doherty (Dobins) and Willie O'Grady (Worms). The first two claimed they were studying the river for eels. 'And do ye think for one instant that I believe ye,' bellowed Noodles 'Do ye think that I believe ye can see the river in the dark and eels at this time of year. Do ye think I came down in the last shower of purest snow. Eels how are ye!" he jeered before going on to Worms O'Grady. 'And I suppose you were shining the lamp for the other two ' he ventured, 'Oh no, Sergeant, as sure as God is me judge sure wasn't I only collecting the worms for the catch whenever that would be. You understand that don't you Sergeant'. said Worms. 'No I certainly do not' bellowed Noodles 'Worms how are you in the middle of the night and with a frost that would bite into the very marrow of your bones.' 'The three of ye are coming with me down to the headquarters immediately,' he went on in a tone of smug satisfaction as if he were onto a decent and worthwhile scent. 'Sergeant Blake you go ahead of us and secure three pairs of handcuffs. They're more than likely in the bottom drawer at the back covered with cobwebs. As you know we have little use for them around these parts, that is until now' he finished as he shot a scurrilous back glance in the direction of Eel, Dobins and Worms. The three had in fact been out at their secret rendezvous tending to their poteen making. In actual fact they were more frightened about being found out in that matter than being inadvertently suspected of Nettles' murder. In any case the three of them were marched down to the local garda station and kept in the custodial charm of Sergeant Nugent.

Part II

It didn't take very long for the trial to come about. And two days later the makeshift courtroom was packed to capacity. Not even a fly could find a spot if indeed a fly could be seen in the cold month of January, so sandwiched together were the bodies of the eager villagers. Judge Sebastian Cripps sat, eyes cast downward, on the old wooden bench which was normally the master's place, for this courtroom was in effect one of the two village classrooms. Acting on their own behalf, the three men were ordered to come forward one at a time for interrogation by an overly confident sergeant Athanasius Nugent. The law in the village of Bruree did not encourage the idea of bringing strange solicitors into private matters that were the concern only of the village itself. And so the trial began, with Noodles in cocksure manner, shooting questions like a firing squad at the three suspects, Eel, Dobins and Worms. Judge Cripps listened carefully and patiently as the local detective continued with his line of questioning. 'And at what time on the night in question did you leave your house?' he asked Eel. "Twas about now, wait till I see" he paused scratching his head by way of dalliance. 'I think maybe,' he stalled 'Twas about quarter past the hour after the Angelus bell rang out'. 'Is that so now?' said the detective 'And did you have anything with you that might conceal a slashook, like a canvas bag maybe.' 'Ah no guard' replied Eel, 'Sure hadn't I only me usual satchel with the bit of bread and tay for the night." 'Then' broke in Noodles 'You intended having a long night did you?' 'That's right' came the prompt reply 'You see the river holds a great attraction for me. I'd stay watching it all night, it does things for me, strange things like you know' 'Yes' snapped Noodles sharply 'Like helping you to plan a murder.' At this vile intrusion on his character Eel took great offence and his face registered total confusion. 'Ah no guard' he replied 'sure I wouldn't hurt a fly everyone knows that' he continued looking for some scrap of assistance from the inquisitive gathering, A few heads were seen to nod in the affirmative, A cough or two was heard to emerge from the silent assemblage. Next in the firing line was Worms 'Tell me' began the detective 'Where were you between the hours of seven o'clock on the night in question and six the following morning?'. 'I was searching for worms, honest guard' he all but stammered. 'And no doubt you took a slashook to aid you in the process, worms how are you in the freezing month of January.' A vacuous silence ensued. Judge Cripps cleared his throat .He didn't appear overly impressed with Nugent's bombastic line of questioning. 'May I ask' he finally broke his silence 'Who it was who first came upon the body of Normoyle?' Molly Muldowney sat in the front row of wooden furoms. She was dressed in her Sunday best. Her black fitted coat with its smart velvet collar, well covered the calves of her black-stockinged slim legs. She wore a black court shoe with a two and a quarter inch heel. Her puce-coloured hat was shot through with a long pin, bearing an emerald studded Celtic design. Her well-brushed silvery hair was totally concealed.

She had not yet recovered from events of the previous two days, her features baring all the signs of a marked strain. 'Your Honour,' replied Detective Sergeant Nugent 'It was Miss Muldowney who first discovered the body.' 'Then in that case' said the judge 'Could I have her up here for questioning?' With that the middle aged woman stood and made her way in confident manner to the makeshift witness box. 'May I ask' began Judge Cripps 'What was your business at the deceased man's house?' 'Yes', replied Miss Muldowney in self-assured manner, 'I was delivering my daily round of duck eggs.' 'And,' continued the judge 'Was the deceased a long-standing customer of yours?" 'Yes sir, he was that for nigh on twenty years now' replied the lady respectfully. 'And did ye ever have a difference in that period of time?' queried Cripps. 'Is it after suspecting me you are sir?" she came back sharply eyeing the Judge with a cautious suspicion in her eyes, a look she normally reserved for her dilatory customers whose payment for her duck eggs consisted of promise after promise. Judge Cripps quickly got the message and giving a slight clearing to his phlemagogic throat adopted another line of questioning. 'Then tell me my good lady,' he ventured, eyeing her over the rim of his thick black-framed glasses, 'What exactly did you encounter when you went to the house of the deceased on the day in question?' My good lady how are you, she thought, isn't it quickly he changes his tune. 'I don't understand the question' she replied pertly. 'And what is it that you don't understand my good lady?' He queried. 'That word' she tried to explain 'It sounds like counter'. 'Oh, oh yes' Cripps replied, trying to resist a very broad grin 'I meant what did you see?' 'Then sir' said the now much more confidant lady, 'You might have said that in the first place. I don't like to be made appear a fool especially in front of my neighbours. Not all are my bosom companions,you know' she added wryly. 'My apologies' the judge mumbled and bade her to continue. 'Well Sir' she now adopted an air of real self-assurance, 'When I opened the outside gate, the first thing that struck me was that the door of the cottage was open. Ned always kept his front door shut, summer and winter'. She paused and looked in the direction of the judge who bade her to continue. "Anyway, as you will remember, we had just had a thick fresh snowfall overnight' she went on. 'As I went in I spotted what I thought were sprinkles of blood here and there. I thought maybe one of the animals might have come to harm during the night'. She stopped. A hushed silence permeated the makeshift courtroom. People sat bolt upright as if eager to hear more. ' And, my good lady' queried the now very interested judge 'Was there anything else that you noticed?" 'Yes,' replied Molly, 'There was something else. I noticed fresh footprints in the snow'. At this point Cripps glanced at Detective Sergeant Nugent who seemed to visibly cringe to half his size. For that glance from the judge seemed to say 'Why the hell didn't you follow up this line of investigation?' 'And tell me Miss Muldowney' the judge continued' Was there anything significant about the footprints' 'Was there anything what?" snapped Molly in the makeshift witness box. 'Oh sorry;' faltered the judge 'did you notice anything special about the footprints? Were they big or small very narrow or very wide?' 'Well now sir, I'd say they were a nine and a half, a good wide fit too' she replied. 'How can you be so sure?" asked the judge 'Don't I know the size too well, isn't the same size as my brother Freddie's. Aren't I buying them for the last twenty–five years, yes I'd say I know the size all too well sir' she replied .By now Detective Sergeant Nugent was emitting uncharacteristic signs of fidgeting, occasioned no doubt by terrible feelings of guilt and inadequacy. Why hadn't he thought of such a simple straightforward type of investigation? The best he could do now was to follow on in the footsteps of Judge Cripps. And tell me the judge went on 'Was there anything else unusual about the footprints?' Could you tell me what you mean now?' asked Miss Muldowney. 'I mean' replied the judge 'Were they long steps or short steps?" 'Oh that,' went on the lady in the witness box 'Well I'll tell you now, they were the footprints of a man with two left feet.' Nugent cringed again in his bench as the judge cast him a swift reprimanding glance. Then returning to his nugget of gold in the witness box, he continued, 'And could you explain further what you mean by two left feet?' 'I can indeed sir', she replied her voice indicating a distinct warming to the unusual looking creature in the wig, 'Wasn't one going easht and the other goin' wesht, that's the way we say it 'round here'. Making a valiant effort yet again to restrain a broad grin Judge Cripps announced 'That will be all for now my good lady you have been worth your weight in gold, thank you'. Then just about raising his eyes to the assembled anxious villagers he mumbled, 'This court is adjourned until further notice.' As the villagers shuffled their noisy way out of the schoolroom, the judge had a quick stiff word with Nuigent. 'I'll give you one week to find the man with the two left feet' he directed and finished 'Do I make myself clear?' as he emitted a cold steely look from out of his frosty eyes.

Within the hour, despite their previous ordeal, Sergeant Nugent called a special meeting with his understudy, Blake. 'We need to spread our wings,' announced the senior man, 'Well have to seek help from the gardai in the nearby villages.' Blake ever ready to row in with Nugent, agreed. The following day, several men in navy blue uniform could be sighted making their way to the village of Bruree; their trousers well fastened to their ankles with the aid of bicycle clips. For the entire world, they looked like the Blue Brigade in swift flight. When they arrived at Garda headquarters in Bruree, Nugent lost no time in taking command of the entire situation. One might say he was into his barrow. And never before having experienced a murder investigation in or around the county before, each and every one of them was full of enthusiasm. 'Now what we are looking for here' begun Nugent 'Is a man with two distinctly left feet who had a motive.' One guard named John McMahon asked 'And what about Eel, Dobbins, and Worms?'. Word of these three suspects had reached the neighbouring villages. 'Unfortunately,' replied Nugent, now really getting the feel of his own importance. 'None of them have the slightest trace of having two left feet. In fact they all possess two distinctive straightforward feet and not one of the three take more that a size eight shoe.' At this disclosure most of them scratched their head as if to indicate, 'Where do we go from here?' Then, out of the awkward silence a voice emerged. It was that of Bartholomew Brady. ' Why don't we go to the scene of the crime and look for any further vital clues'he piped up. Everyone there seemed to register agreement. Detective Sargeant Nugent thought it was a great idea. Blake also did. So it was decided there and then that he himself, Blake, Brady and one other Ferret Franklin, would go to the scene of the murder. The gathering disassembled and all adjourned for a pint of Guinness to Pa Frawley's pub before cycling back to their own villages.

That evening Noodles, Blake, Brady and Ferret made their eager way to the house of the murdered man, who by now incidentally was buried, the new gravedigger being a brawny young man named Alexis Stewart. Cautiously they entered the house. It was clearly obvious on first sight that poor old Nettles didn't have much by way of these worlds' comforts. A kind of pallyass formed the place where he slept. He didn't even allow himself the comfort of an oil lamp. Instead he settled for candles. He had a store of them in the bottom drawer of his self-made meagre dresser. What the guard wasn't aware of was that most of the candle storage came compliments of the church. But then how were they to know the difference between altar candles which were special long-burning, from the ordinary household candle. Following much meticulous rooting about, Brady swooped upon a cigarette case .Now, no ordinary cigarette case was this but sleek and slim and wonder of wonders, it was made of rolled gold. Unfortunately it didn't have any initials on it. It was common knowledge that Nettles never smoked, for it was incumbent on him to keep fit, otherwise he would not have been equal to the his back-breaking job. So to whom did the cigarette case containing nine 'Sweet Afton' belong to? Whoever it was, they surmised, must have inadvertently tossed out the cigarette case in his fumbling efforts to find his lighter. For the foursome had agreed that the place must have been in complete darkness when he carried out his deadly, gruesome act. 'I know what we'll do' said Blake, by far the deepest thinker of the four, 'We'll take it to the antique dealer, maybe he can shed some light on it.' The lighter obviously was an exceptionally good make and to the ordinary person would have passed for pure gold. The owner was clearly a man of wealth. Maybe the expensive cigarette case was even purchased at that very antique shop. Upon further investigation they learned that one Julian Simington had opened an antique shop in the past three months in the nearby town of. Charleville. The owner was reputed to be a most astute purveyor of antiques. His shop was aptly called, 'The Gold Nugget'. Sergeant Nugent decided that he and Blake would pay a visit to these premises and no time was to be lost in so doing. The following morning, even before the early fog had lifted, the investigating duo cycled along the bumpy road to Charleville, their front lamps alight and their rear reflectors poised to illuminate on the approach from behind of any early morning vehicle. This was an errand of most urgent importance, that could win or loose them much prestige in the garda force. Arriving at their destination much too early for opening time, they whiled away the time by attending Mass at the local church. After Mass, they made their way up to 'The Gold Nugget'. They arrived just in time to find a very business-like man in his early thirties removing wooden shutters from the front of the premises. The shop window was packed full with all sorts of precious gems, from slim silver and gold cigarette lighters to the most unusual bronze figurines.

Almost immediately Blake observed what he considered a significant fact but let on nothing to the senior detective sergeant. Both men walked in after the proprietor as he briskly carried one of the green painted shutters inside. He seemed to pale ever so slightly upon facing the two gardai. Both men, however, put this down to a common nervousness on the part of most antique dealers. They were ever conscious of mistakenly buying in stolen goods. Then slipping his right hand into his left inside pocket, Nugent produced the rolled-gold cigarette case. Upon doing so, both men of the law observed a distinct change in the manner, if not mannerism of Julian Simington. He fidgeted about, moving things, only to replace them in the selfsame place again. 'Can you tell us' broached the senior garda, 'What type of man might purchase this kind of cigarette case?' 'Oh that that kind,' waved Simington, 'I suppose he'd be in the upper income bracket, a man who would probably own a very big house and, maybe have a servant or two. A real aristocrat, yes, I'd wager a very aristocratic type.' Simington, they observed was a man of some six feet, of slim build, fair to mousy hair and a well-cultured moustache. His swift, efficient movements gave all the appearances of a very slick man. He had little time for dawdling, and gave out very direct signals that he wished to get on with the business of the day and that these two men of the law were definitely putting an obstacle in the way of that process. Brady, wishing to confirm what he was sure he had already observed asked Simington the price of the jewellery box that was displayed in the window. Simington, with all the suavity of a man in command of his own business strode swiftly across the floor and over to the window where the jewellery box was displayed. Brady nudged Nugent. Brady then walked over and handled the item, giving the appearance of a most interested would be purchaser. 'Beautiful' he observed 'must come by when it comes closer to my wife's birthday'. With a feeling of satisfaction Simington replaced the jewel box on the window again. Appearing somewhat more relaxed he seemed to revert to his old self.

Leaving 'The Gold Nugget', both men of the law displayed very little haste. They just strolled down the road, rolling their bicycles. But once past the bend of the road they mounted their two-wheeled machines and pedalled like the hammers of hell back to the headquarters in Bruree. By now both men were fully conscious of one fact, Julian Simington the antique dealer and proprietor of 'The Gold Nugget' had two very distinct left feet that could easily have been size nine or nine and a half. The next thing they would have to ascertain was why would such a man want to kill Nettles Normoyle. ? One might say, that they had a successfully overed a giant hurdle only to run blindly into a blank wall. The very next day, a second meeting of all the gardai from the neighbouring towns and villages convened. The bare facts were laid before them. It was now necessary for someone of superior intelligence to unravel this difficult knot, someone who could possibly get into the mind of Julian Simington. Unfortunately nothing worthwhile emerged from their meeting that day. The following day, Blake having had time to sleep on it and having several times invoked the help of the Holy Spirit, approached Nugent with a bright idea. And this was how he placed the fact before his senior, 'The man whom Nettles buried that day, one Anselm Thornhill, wasn't he a particularly rich man? 'That's right', replied Nugent in a casual manner, totally unimpressed by what his colleague considered to be a major disclosure. Undaunted, however, Blake continued 'Didn't he go to his grave with an amount of jewellery and I mean jewellery of a superior quality, possibly from a bygone age?'. Removing his glasses Nugent cleared his throat and shot a sudden awakening glance at his understudy. 'You mean' he said 'there could be a motive after all?' 'That there could' replied Blake, 'You see you should rely more on the Holy Spirit'. This was the first time in the history of their five-year working relationship that Blake ventured to tell Nugent he should do anything. 'You know' said the senior detective 'you could have a point there, we'll have to seek further'. And seek they did and discovered much. They found that Julian Simington was every bit the slick individual he appeared to be. He possessed an insatiable greed for money and was prepared to go to any lengths to satisfy that greed.

As the days progressed, Nugent and Blake discovered that one gombeen at least, was willing to participate in his evil doings. That was a big, brawny chap of only twenty-four years of age. His name was Ferdie Tomkins. He was reputed to have the strength of an ox, with overly developed forearms from working the plough with his father Dan. A rather jovial fellow by nature, he was well liked by all the people in Kilmallock, where he lived but a few miles outside. But few if any were aware of his occasional nocturnal activities or of his unsavoury involvement with the antique dealer Julian Simington. What eventually led the gardai to Ferdie was the fact that, upon conversing with the villagers, they deduced that he was one of the few strangers who happened to attend the wake of Anselm Thornhill. But as was in the case of every village or town, someone knew him. But for all his outstanding physical strength, however Ferdie wasn't the very brightest of young men, and Simington was quick to spot him as an excellent prospect for his devilish deeds. For, it soon emerged, when the guard questioned Ferdie, that he was actually Simington's henchman. It seemed that Simington was in the habit of keeping a close eye on the death columns of the local newspapers, and often further afield. He had his own ways and means of discovering whether or not the deceased was a person of wealth. He was also self-informed of the various gravediggers that might be involved. After all, it was to his own advantage, for ventures such as these could mean big business to him. In any case he stayed very much out of the picture. It was left to poor Ferdie to attend the wakes in order to observe well the fingers of the deceased, be they male or female. 'Take note,' Simington would caution Ferdie, 'See if they have rings of any worth and also take note if the family have left any precious item in the coffin that they had wished to take with them to the grave. Observe boy, observe well!' It was also Ferdie's business to get to know any of the gravediggers. Most of the gravediggers were drawn into the unsavoury net by the promises of a few half crowns. It was usually a day or two following the internment that Ferdie would approach the gravediggers with the proposition. Then, that night, both gravediggers would go to the cemetery and work like troopers to empty the grave of the soft earth. With the aid of a tool they would unscrew the lid of the coffin. Within a matter of seconds the precious jewellery or other ornate items would be removed and placed securely in a black draw-string purse, which was safely deposited in Ferdie's inside coat pocket. Ferdie never faltered. Neither did he help himself. In truth he was too stupid not to be honest. On the following day the entire legacy would be passed on to Simington. No gravedigger was ever the wiser of the said Julian Simington. He was, what one would call nowadays, the all –powerful , invisible, godfather!

When he was sounded by the gardai, Ferdie innocently let out everything. Never before having had a brush with the law, he judged himself to be in real trouble. But as it emerged he was put down as an innocent victim caught in the jaws of a very wise and lethal shark.

Two days later, the trial re-convened. The verdict was a foregone conclusion. Julian Simington, without the shadow of a doubt was found guilty of the murder of poor old Nettles Normoyle. For, when Ferdie had approached Nettles on the deal, the poor, honest gravedigger wouldn't comply. Ferdie then reported the matter to Simington, who, being fearful that nettles might tell, took care of matters in his own cruel and deadly way. One might say, in trying to outwit the gravedigger, he became trapped in the inextricable net of his own insatiable greed. He lived to regret never having taken his mothers advice to straighten out those two left feet or you'll be marked for life, mark my words!. He seemed to recall that one of his teachers, a nun named Sr. Bonaventura, had issued the selfsame warning, particularly during practise for First Holy Communion.